A CHANCE ENCOUNTER

When Grace Maxwell swerves to avoid a dog that runs out in front of her car, the near miss begins a chain of events that leads her to Daniel Stafford. At the college ball, Melissa Harper, Daniel's fiancée, had discovered Grace and Daniel kissing, and she had broken off their engagement . . . Grace now works as a vet's receptionist and to make matters worse Daniel takes over the practice. Then she learns Melissa Harper is back on the scene . . .

MARGARET MOUNSDON

A CHANCE ENCOUNTER

Complete and Unabridged

LINFORD
Leicester

First published in Great Britain in 2011

First Linford Edition
published 2012

British Library CIP Data

Mounsdon, Margaret.
   A chance encounter. - -
   (Linford romance library)
   1. Love stories.
   2. Large type books.
   I. Title II. Series
   823.9'2–dc23

   ISBN 978–1–4448–1325–8

Published by
F. A. Thorpe (Publishing)
Anstey, Leicestershire

Set by Words & Graphics Ltd.
Anstey, Leicestershire
Printed and bound in Great Britain by
T. J. International Ltd., Padstow, Cornwall

This book is printed on acid-free paper

An Unlucky Moment

Grace Maxwell bowled down the country lane in her nippy new car, singing along to the radio. She had always loved the song that was playing and, as the first crocuses of spring pushed through the damp winter earth, she felt glad to be alive.

It hadn't been an easy time for her recently, one way or another. Charlie was still a drain on her finances, even though he promised he was trying to sort them out, but today, Grace decided, was a fresh start. She had come through all the bad bits and things could only get better.

She had a job she loved and people were finally beginning to forget her past. Her little car purred happily as she took the sharp bend carefully. Grace knew from experience you were likely to come across the unexpected in the heart of the country, from skittish horses to diffident deer. She had seen it all and she wasn't about to dent her shiny paintwork for lack of attention to the road.

The way ahead was clear and Grace increased the pressure on the accelerator. She could smell spring in the air.

Grace didn't see the small bundle of black fur dart out in front of her until it was almost too late. She swerved and pressed down hard on the brakes as she lost control of the steering wheel. Her car turned round in a complete circle before it slewed to a halt in the ditch facing the wrong direction. She coughed as the smell of hot rubber scorched the road and caught the back of her throat.

Fumbling for the door, she grabbed the handle, but it wouldn't budge. The window was still open and seizing her chance she managed to wriggle through the gap and topple out on to the grassy verge. Fighting for breath, she took a few moments to steady her nerves.

The dog — she looked round

frantically as her heartbeat returned to normal. Where was it? Prone as she was on the grass she could see it wasn't lying injured under the car. A whine from the ditch attracted her attention. She swivelled round. Two pathetic brown eyes looked up at her. The animal shivered in fear and shrank away from her as she reached out to touch it.

'It's all right,' she crooned. 'I won't hurt you.'

A tentative pink tongue licked her fingers. Grace knew better than to make any sudden movements, but she had to see if the poor thing was injured. Soft whiskers tickled her fingertips as she let the dog grow used to her smell and touch.

'There's a good boy. Now are you going to let me take a look at you?'

With the tiniest of squeaks the dog permitted her to put her hands around his still shivering body. The silky fur was damp, but thankfully not with blood.

'I think I missed you, don't you?' She smiled into the soulful eyes. 'You're just a bit shaken up like me, aren't you? Come on.'

To her relief the dog began scrabbling towards her. Moments later her crisp white blouse was bespattered with mud as the animal shook the moisture off its fur.

'We'd better get you to the vet's, don't you think?' she suggested, glad she'd had the foresight to grab up her bag on the way out of the driver's window. 'You're lucky I work for him, aren't you, and that I was on my way to work?'

★   ★   ★

No harm done.' Mr Vincent turned off his inspection light and patted the recumbent animal. 'I wish the same could be said of you.'

Grace had not realised she was sporting a colourful bruise from where her forehead had come into contact with the windscreen, until the mechanic who had been dispatched from the local garage arrived to rescue her car from the ditch.

'Have an argument with a horse, did you?' he asked inspecting the car in the ditch. 'Boss mentioned something about an animal.'

'It was this little chap.' Grace looked down at the dog she was still cradling in her arms. 'He ran out in front of me.'

'Some people shouldn't own animals,' the mechanic replied, 'if they can't look after them. Reckon he belongs to one of that towny lot over there, don't you?'

He nodded in the direction of where a new estate had recently been built.

'They're out all day doing something important in their offices, with no respect for the countryside or time for their pets.' He grinned at her. 'You do look a sight and no mistake.'

Grace rubbed at her bump. 'Hopefully it will go down in a couple of days.'

Now, feeling the egg-sized protuberance on her forehead, she wasn't so sure.

'All the same,' Mr Vincent the vet

advised her after he'd finished dealing with the dog and expressed a similar opinion to that of the car mechanic's, 'it might be a wise move to get the doctor to take a look at you.'

'I'll call in at the chemist on my way home, it's nothing some arnica won't cure,' Grace insisted.

'Well, off you go. I'll look after this little chap. I can see a metal disc attached to his collar with a number on it. Seems his name is Foxy.' He tweaked one of Foxy's ears. 'Best get you reunited with your owner, hadn't we?' He peered at Grace over his bifocals. 'I'll also be giving Foxy's owner a piece of my mind. I can't afford to have my receptionist off work due to an accident that need never have happened.'

'I'll stay until the end of my shift,' Grace offered, ignoring the throbbing pain in her head.

'You'll do no such thing. I can manage. You get yourself off home. When will your car be back on the road?'

6

'The garage wanted to check it through so hopefully I'll have it back tomorrow.'

'Would you like to borrow my bicycle?'

Grace had worked for Mr Vincent for four years now and she loved it. No day was the same. It was a dream job being the receptionist at his vet's practice.

She knew practically everyone in the village and the surgery was a hub of local activity. The notice board in the waiting room was officially for professional purposes, but Grace had never been able to refuse requests for clients wanting to sell guinea pigs or rabbits or find a home for newborn kittens.

'How will you get home?' Grace asked.

'I'll call my wife to come and collect me. I have one or two bits of paperwork I need to catch up on.' His blue eyes twinkled.

Grace smiled back at him. Although he was many years her senior, from her first day, Grace sensed a bond between the two of them. She respected his years of experience looking after injured animals, worried pets and even more worried owners.

He and his wife had also been there for Grace after the bottom had dropped out of her world. These days they were more than friends they were her family.

'See you in the morning then?' She smiled back at Mr Vincent. 'I may be a little late as I'll need to collect my car.'

Mr Vincent waved at her and went off to answer the telephone.

'Bye, Foxy,' she said to the still recumbent dog. There was a gentle thud as he wagged his tail on the inspection table.

★ ★ ★

'My goodness.' Amelia MacPherson tutted as Grace pushed open the door to the post office after she'd parked Mr Vincent's bicycle round the back of the shed. 'What happened to you?'

Grace was now sporting a colourful bruise that was beginning spread and turn an interesting shade of dark purple.

'It really not as bad as it looks,' she insisted after she had explained the day's events over a cup of tea in the little back room.

'Well, I prescribe a nice hot bath then an early night.'

'Won't you need me to cover in the shop?' she asked.

'Certainly not. Beattie and I will cope. Would you like to join us for supper? It's our speciality, home-made shepherd's pie with cheesy crust mashed potato. I know it's one of your favourites.'

'I couldn't,' Grace began to protest, her mouth watering at the prospect.

'Nonsense.' Miss MacPherson was having none of it. 'You go and have a long soak. There's plenty of hot water and a new packet of my pine crystals. They do wonders for aching limbs. Help yourself then come down when you're ready.'

Grace's little room was no more than a cubbyhole under the eaves, but she had the use of the whole of the top floor of the old post house. She shared a large Victorian bathroom with Miss MacPherson and her widowed sister, Beattie Bishop, who both lived on the floor below.

It was a convenient arrangement. For a modest rent Grace was allowed the use of all their facilities and the tiny back garden, in exchange for the occasional stint in the shop. Amelia and her sister needed cover of an early evening or Saturday mornings when they liked to have a lie-in. Grace didn't mind getting up early at weekends and opening up the shop for the newspaper deliveries and taking in the milk and bread.

She fingered the bump. The arnica had brought out the worst of her bruise, but there was no denying she was going to have a shiner in the morning.

She didn't doubt news of her accident would get round and there would be a constant stream of visitors to tomorrow's surgery. Working in both the surgery and the general stores, Grace was a well-known figure in the local community. She smiled. Some people would object to having their life the centre of gossip, but Grace didn't mind. She'd grown up as the centre of gossip and she knew these days it was the villagers' way of expressing their concern for her welfare.

She inhaled the steamy pine fragrance and squeezed hot water from her sponge onto her aching limbs. She was lucky there had only been minor damage to her car — a bent bumper and the mechanic thought her tracking might need adjustment which he told her he would have to inspect in the pit.

These days Grace did not have a private allowance and she realised now how her changed circumstances had made her a much nicer person.

'What a little spoilt prig I must have been in the past,' she muttered as she poured more hot water in the bath, remembering how unreasonable she used to be in her demands before life had taught her a serious lesson.

A few years ago the idea of actually working for her living would have filled her with horror. If work had been necessary, she would probably have undertaken light duties at the golf club, or an art gallery, something like that, nothing too strenuous. Getting up at four or five of a Saturday morning would have sent her into meltdown.

She grinned. The strange thing was she had never been happier in her life. Now she had purpose to her life and she knew people were nice to her because they liked her, not because she was the daughter of Duncan Maxwell.

'Grace?' Amelia MacPherson called up the stairs. 'Five minutes.'

'Coming,' Grace called out.

She could smell the fragrant cheese of the shepherd's pie crust wafting up the stairs. With all the upset, she had eaten no more than half a sandwich all day and she was really hungry. That was another thing about her that had changed. In the past all she ever did was toy with a few pieces of salad. Now she had the heartiest appetite of anyone she knew and she absolutely adored jacket potatoes with lashings of butter and grated cheese.

'Anything I can do?' she asked as she strolled into the back kitchen five minutes later.

'Would you like to strain the carrots? Beattie is just shutting up the hens.'

'They're all right for the night,' Beattie said as she locked the back door. 'Good grief.' She caught sight of Grace's bruises. 'Amelia told me you had a bump on the head, but I wasn't expecting anything quite so impressive or colourful.' Her weather beaten face was full of concern. 'How did it happen?'

After Grace updated Beattie on the day's events and they had eaten their supper, the three of them shared a pot of tea at the kitchen table. Amelia dunked her favourite digestive biscuits while her sister and Grace munched on some chocolate fingers.

'I heard a piece of news in the library today,' Beattie Bishop announced. 'I hope it won't distress you too much, Grace.'

'Distress me?' she frowned. 'What's happened?'

'Sycamore House has been sold.'

Upsetting News

Daniel Stafford finished his telephone call with a frown. It was not a good start. Foxy had never run away before. He could only suppose the lure of exciting new smells had been too much for the dog's investigative nature.

Daniel had spent two hours searching for Foxy before he had been forced to give up. He was only pleased there hadn't been a serious accident. From what the vet had said, it sounded as though his receptionist had been involved. He'd get her details he decided when he called in to pick up Foxy and send her a bunch of flowers as a gesture of apology.

He sat down at the desk and went through his paperwork again. It had been a big decision to move back to this part of Sussex. Five years ago, he'd shaken the dust of Fieldling off his feet

15

and moved away. It had been a clean break and he had enjoyed his five years travelling, first around the world, then when the glamour of constantly living out of a suitcase began to pall he had moved back home and taken on mobile work.

His years on the road had taught him a lot about how the countryside worked and its specific requirements. Although he was Sussex born and bred, his knowledge of working farms had been limited to theory. There was, he decided, nothing like practice to get hands on experience of the problems of their day-to-day life.

He had nursed every type of animal from newly birthed lambs to elderly dogs. He loved the look of trust in their eyes and did his best to preserve their dignity no matter the circumstances.

Daniel's father had come from farming stock and, although he had died when Daniel was a boy, he suspected he had inherited his father's genes. He had always loved animals and hated to see them in distress, and that was why the telephone call from the local vet had disturbed him.

He fully accepted he was at fault in the matter and should have kept a closer eye on Foxy, but to hear someone refer to him as an unthinking towny had upset him. He needed to gain the local people's trust and this was not a good start.

It was also a very unfortunate coincidence that it should have been the vet who had made the call. When he had discovered his identity, Mr Vincent had sounded as surprised as Daniel had been to receive his call. The older man had not recognised his telephone number and for the first few minutes of their exchange had not realised to whom he was speaking.

A clock ticked comfortingly in the background as Daniel went back to his notes to check them through one last time. This could be the most important decision of his life and he did not want to overlook any detail, no matter how small.

It had been the same when he'd

taken the plunge and bought Sycamore House. When it had first come on the market he had debated whether or not to express an interest in the property. It held no particular memory for him, but he appreciated it had a chequered history.

An industrialist had originally purchased it for his family. Over the years it had changed hands several times, then the previous owners had bought it purely as a commercial venture. It had fallen into neglect and needed significant tender loving care to restore it to its former glory.

The gardens were still in want of attention, but the house was a reflection of the many hours of hard work dedicated to its refurbishment. It wasn't that big a house, but Daniel was the first to admit it was on the large side for a single man with only a spaniel for company.

He supposed his sister would visit from time to time bringing her brood with her, but apart from the visits from his daily, he was mostly on his own.

In the summer there would be the garden to work on of course and during the day if things went according to plan he would be out much of the time. All the same, it was the first time he had lived totally on his own, a situation that would take some getting used to.

The estate agent had described it as a character property, and Daniel supposed that was exactly what it was. It was set in the heart of the village with a large rear garden that boasted spectacular views of the surrounding countryside.

The house itself was quite compact and, due to the oak beams, warm and welcoming. So far he had only managed on basic furnishings but he decided there would be plenty of time in the coming months to decide exactly what he was going to do with the various rooms at his disposal.

Sycamore House had been built in the early part of the last century and, whilst great attention had been paid to the structure and foundations, the rooms themselves could only be described as unstructured. No two were the same and although that was part of their charm, Daniel suspected he would have a challenge on his hands when it came to sorting out décor and colour schemes, not an area he was familiar with.

He glanced at his watch. His appointment was for the early afternoon. There was time for a shower and a quick freshen up, he decided, before his meeting.

* * *

'Foxy's still here?' Grace was greeted by the little dog, which raced towards her barking recognition as she entered the office.

'His owner's coming to collect him after lunch,' Mr Vincent explained. 'Foxy seems to have suffered no lasting side effects from yesterday's experience. How are you feeling?'

'Much better after a good night's sleep.'

'My wife was most concerned to hear of your accident. I think if you hadn't been in such good hands with the ladies at the post house, she would have insisted you spend the night with us.'

'Thank you,' Grace said, touched by his kindness.

She suspected that since their son and daughter had both moved to New Zealand, Mr and Mrs Vincent missed the bustle of family life and there was nothing more Mrs Vincent would have liked than to have someone to fuss around.

'Have we got a busy day?' Grace asked looking around the unusually quiet surgery. 'Where is everybody?'

'Actually,' Mr Vincent cleared his throat, 'I've deliberately kept today free of appointments, apart from emergencies.'

'Not because of me? Grace asked feeling guilty.

Yesterday had been a rare first day off for her. She loved her work so much Mr Vincent had almost to force her to take a holiday.

'The thing is ... ' Mr Vincent paused. 'Perhaps you'd better come through to the office.'

'What's going on?' Grace asked, now experiencing a shiver of unease. It was unlike Mr Vincent to be so secretive. 'You're not ill, are you?'

'No, nothing like that.' Mr Vincent took his time sitting down at his desk. 'I don't really know where to start.'

By now Grace's nerves were at screaming point. Mr Vincent's kindly face showed he was in an agony of indecision.

'My wife and I have decided after much reflection to join our family in New Zealand.'

'You're emigrating?'

'This last winter has been an extremely busy one and to be honest I'm not as young as I used to be. I don't find the call-outs any easier. As you know, we are the only local practice and the workload can sometimes be demanding.'

'That's because you provide such good service,' Grace pointed out. 'You always go the extra mile and people appreciate that.'

'I love my work, but Mrs Vincent misses the grandchildren and she has been very supportive in the past when our home life has been disrupted due to my work. I really feel it's time to hand over the reins to someone younger.'

'I see.' Grace was aware of a small warm body nudging hers. She bent down and picking up Foxy cuddled him. He licked her face.

'He's an engaging little fellow, isn't he?' Mr Vincent smiled. 'Actually, it was rather embarrassing.'

'What was?' Grace asked, not really paying attention to what Mr Vincent had to say. Her brain was still reeling from the shock of his news.

'I telephoned the number on the disc on his collar and I'm afraid I didn't mince my words. I accused the poor man who answered of all sorts of manner of neglect. I suppose I was worried about you and how the accident could have had far worse repercussions.

'He was most apologetic and as I ran out of steam, I realised it was him.'

'What was him?' Grace asked with a frown, aware she hadn't been paying much attention to what Mr Vincent had been saying.

'The new man, or rather the man I hope will be taking my place here.'

'You've already got a replacement?' Mr Vincent now had Grace's full attention.

'I am sorry I couldn't break the news to you earlier, Grace, but if things had fallen through, I could have alarmed you unnecessarily. You do understand, don't you?'

'Of course,' Grace answered in a husky voice. There was a whimper from Foxy as she squeezed him a bit too hard. 'Sorry,' she whispered into his ear.

'We hope to firm up details this afternoon. We have an appointment after lunch. You'll be able to meet him then. He's a young man with lots of progressive ideas. I'm sure I've been a bit blinkered when it comes to modern technology. I've been a believer in the old saying 'if it ain't broke, don't fix it' school of thinking.' He smiled. 'But I do realise some of my practices are a little outdated. We are sadly in need of a makeover.'

Grace knew with conviction that the absolutely last person she wanted to see in this world was Mr Vincent's replacement.

'That's not true. Our style suits Fieldling. People don't want a state-of-the-art surgery. They want honest plain service and that's what they get here.'

'I agree, but I feel it's time to move on. If I leave it any longer, it will be too late to emigrate and that wouldn't be fair on Mrs Vincent.'

'When is this new man coming in to see you, did you say?'

'Two-thirty this afternoon. I thought we could have our meeting in here then you could perhaps show him your side of things?'

'Will he want to keep me on as a receptionist?'

'I have given you a glowing reference.'

'If he's as modern as you say, won't he want someone blonde and decorative?'

These days Grace knew her appearance was more working girl than the glamorous model-like creature she had once been.

'If he's got any sense he'll keep you on, Grace. I've left him in no doubt of the high regard I have for your capabilities and I don't think a blonde and decorative assistant would be keen on getting her hands dirty.'

'He may look into my . . . ' Grace hesitated ' . . . background.'

Mr Vincent felt a pang of sympathy for the slender girl seated in front of him. Life had dealt her a series of hard blows when first her father had died, then her world had come crashing down around her after it was discovered they were living on borrowed earnings and there was no way any of them could be paid back.

Grace had gone from a pampered existence of ponies, a private pool and parties every weekend, to a room above the post office and having to work for her living. Her brother, Charlie, had not fared so well and flitted from job to job, occasionally turning up in the village when yet another of his schemes had crashed and needing to borrow money from his sister.

As for her mother, Teresa Maxwell, she had never been a woman to be on her own for very long, and last year she had remarried. She was now Madame LeGrand. She and her new husband, Philippe, ran a small bed and breakfast establishment outside Nice.

At first she had been the subject of much hurtful gossip as the collapse of her father's business empire had affected several local lives, but gradually people developed a grudging respect for the way Grace kept her dignity and worked hard to rebuild her life.

The day she had knocked on Mr Vincent's door was one he remembered well. She had been desperate for work after being forced to leave college without any qualifications.

'I'll do anything,' she implored, 'sweep floors, make the tea, clean the surgery. Please.' She grasped his arm. 'Miss MacPherson told me your previous receptionist was retiring. I'll work for peanuts. Just give me a chance. I promise you won't regret it.'

It had been Mr Vincent's first inclination to send her away as her father's activities had inadvertently been the reason his son had moved to New Zealand. Mr Vincent's son's business had collapsed as part of the fallout that followed Mr Maxwell's untimely death and as there was no future for him in England he had moved to the other side of the world.

Then Mr Vincent saw the desperation in the girl's pale blue eyes and his heart went out to her. If his daughter, heaven forbid, should ever find herself in a similar situation, he hoped someone would give her a chance.

'Very well.' He nodded. 'Would a month's trial suit you?'

He had not been prepared for almost being knocked off his feet as Grace threw her arms round his neck and kissed him.

'Thank you, thank you,' she gabbled.

'Start tomorrow. Eight o'clock sharp,' he said, wondering if he would see her again.

'I won't let you down,' Grace promised.

From that day neither of them had looked back. Grace had settled to the job of receptionist and Mr Vincent discovered what a pleasure it was to have someone reliable to take messages and to look after his patients while he was out on his rounds.

'You have nothing to be ashamed of in your background, Grace,' he said in a soft voice.

'Not everyone would agree with you,' Grace replied equally quietly.

'What happened to your family was a long time ago. I don't think your lack of official qualifications would hold you back now. There are many people in the village who would be more than pleased to endorse my references.'

Grace bit down a small sigh. It was kind of Mr Vincent to say so, but she didn't know if she believed him. There was still a hard core who refused to forget.

She glanced at the disc on Foxy's collar and stiffened.

'Isn't that the telephone number of Sycamore House?' she asked.

'Yes.'

'So the new owner lives there?'

'He has bought the property. Yes.'

'Beattie Bishop was telling us over supper last night that someone new had moved in.'

'You don't miss your old family home?' Mr Vincent asked.

'Not any more,' Grace admitted. 'In the beginning it was hard as I had to walk by it every day, but now I hardly ever think about it. It's as if it belonged to another life.'

Her smile was a little on the shaky side. If the truth were told she did occasionally regret having to move out. It had been a wonderful family home and her old life had been idyllic.

Every weekend there were tennis parties and barbecues in the summer and ski-ing holidays and visits to glamorous sunspots during the winter months. Her father had been a very sociable man and Grace and her brother had not wanted for any luxury. It had been a dreadful shock when she had been thrown out into the real world.

'I shall look forward to meeting this new man.' Grace gave Mr Vincent a reassuring smile. Her personal life was not his problem. 'And you mustn't worry about me. You know I'm a survivor. You and Mrs Vincent will have a wonderful time in New Zealand and I shall expect an invitation to visit.'

'Of course,' Mr Vincent replied with a look of relief. 'These days it's so easy to keep in touch with people even when they live on the far side of the world. It will be as if I'm still here. We can talk on the computer and I'll send you lots of pictures and I know my wife will not want to lose contact.'

'I shall miss you,' Grace said, smiling into his kindly face, 'but it's time to move on and talking of moving on, I suppose I had better make sure yesterday's paperwork is up to date,' Grace said as she stood up. 'Especially if there's going to be an inspection.' She turned in the doorway. 'By the way, what is the new man's name?'

'Stafford.'

'Daniel Stafford?' Grace asked in a shaky voice hoping for a negative reply.

'That's the man. He used to live in the area, but after he qualified he went off to do other things. Now he's back. Actually, you might know him. I should imagine you moved in the same social circles.'

Grace's hold on the doorknob tightened.

'Yes,' she said in a tight voice, 'I know

Daniel Stafford.' The bump on her head began to throb painfully.

'Good.' Mr Vincent beamed at her. 'In that case you'll be able to catch up on old times, won't you?'

'I very much doubt it,' Grace muttered under her breath. It was fortunate Mr Vincent's hearing wasn't all it should be, she thought, as she made her way to her desk.

Daniel Stafford was possibly the last man she ever wanted to see again and as for him keeping her on as receptionist, the idea was laughable.

Memories Are Stirred

By the time two o'clock came round Grace was feeling physically sick. She had been unable to eat any lunch and was forced to tell Mr Vincent her lack of appetite was an after effect of the accident.

'Why don't you take the afternoon off?' he asked. 'I'm sure Mr Stafford would understand. You could meet up with him another time.'

'No,' Grace said firmly. It would only delay the moment of confrontation and Daniel had to know about her sometime. It was better to get things over with sooner rather than later.

'Well, sit quietly for a while. I'll make us a pot of tea, shall I?' Mr Vincent offered. 'Then I'll be in the workshop if you need me. Let me know when Mr Stafford arrives.'

Grace nodded glad to have the

opportunity of being on her own for a while. There were so many thoughts buzzing through her brain, she needed time to calm them down. She wished she wasn't sporting a huge bruise on her forehead and the beginnings of a black eye. It was hardly the professional image she wanted to portray to the man whose love life she had ruined, even if she had received her injuries rescuing his dog.

Grace chewed at the top of a pencil. How would she ever forget the night of the prom ball? She remembered it as if were yesterday. She and Melissa Harper had been looking forward to it for weeks. They had hired special gowns and spent all day getting their hair extensions and nails done.

Then at the last moment Melissa had told her she wouldn't be travelling with the rest of the girls in the especially ordered luxury car Grace's father had booked, because she was bringing her fiancé. To say the announcement had created a stir was something of an understatement.

'You're only eighteen,' Grace had protested.

'So?' Melissa had challenged her. 'Jealous?'

'Of course not.' Grace was only annoyed she hadn't thought to bring along a boyfriend of her own to show off to Melissa.

There was no end of young men she could have persuaded into accompanying her. Duncan Maxwell's personable daughter was never short of admirers. Now she would be forced to travel with a bunch of silly giggling girls. In a fit of pique she had made her father cancel the limousine and got her mother to drive her to the ball in solitary splendour.

Later, beset by contrition, Grace realised how badly she was behaving and personally apologised to her friends for ruining the start of their evening. Several of them chose to turn their backs on her. Overcome with remorse Grace had stumbled from the ballroom.

Tripping on the steps she had fallen into a steadying pair of male arms.

She found herself staring into the most handsome male face she had ever seen. Concerned hazel eyes looked down into hers.

'Are you all right?'

The voice matched the eyes. It was rich and deep and sent shivers up Grace's spine.

'Yes, thank you.'

'No, you're not. You're crying.'

Grace could never cry prettily. She knew girls who could turn crying into an art form. When she cried her eyes went all pink and her face turned blotchy. She tried to push him away.

'I can't leave you like this,' he insisted. 'Why don't we walk down to the lake and you can tell me what's upsetting you?'

He must have taken her hiccup of surprise for assent because the next thing Grace knew they were strolling across the lawn of the country club down to the boating lake. The night air was deliciously cool and she began to feel better.

'I don't know your name,' she said overcome with unusual shyness.

'Daniel Stafford.'

'I'm Grace Maxwell.'

'Are you a student?'

'Media studies,' she replied.

'Another hopeful actress?' He could hear amused tolerance in his voice.

'It's not about acting.' She raised her voice, annoyed at his superior stance. 'Anyway, what do you do? I haven't seen you around college.'

'That's because I'm not a student. I'm here as a guest.'

'Shouldn't you be getting back to your partner?'

'All in good time,' he replied.

They sat down on one of the benches bordering the lake.

'How old are you?' she asked.

'Twenty-one. I won't ask you the same question because it's rude to ask a lady her age, isn't it?'

'I haven't been particularly ladylike

this evening,' Grace admitted. 'In fact, I've behaved appallingly.'

'Surely not.'

'I tried apologising to my friends, but they wouldn't listen.'

'That bad, was it?'

'Yes.'

'And that's why you hurled out of the doors like a rocket on lift off?'

'Sort of,' Grace admitted. 'It's so difficult to apologise when you're in the wrong, isn't it?'

'Takes courage and it's even worse when it gets thrown back in your face. So what did you do that was so terrible?'

Grace acquainted him with the facts of the case, not bothering to present herself in a favourable light. He would probably find out about the incident anyway later on.

'Poor you,' he sympathised. 'Still at least you've tried to make amends.'

'Why don't you tell me something terrible you've done?' Grace asked, 'to ease my conscience?'

'Now there's a question.' Daniel frowned and took a few moments out to consider his answer. 'I did once try to smoke a cigarette behind the bike sheds at school.'

'What was it like?'

'Disgusting. The school sneak found me and I got suspended which was the pits as I missed my sixth form prom completely.'

His reply made Grace laugh and she began to feel better.

'Actually, the incident did me a favour. I've never smoked another cigarette in my life and I never will.'

'Now we've confessed everything to each other perhaps we'd better go back inside,' Grace suggested. 'Your date will be wondering what's happened to you.'

'That's a very pretty dress you're wearing.' Daniel moved in closer to her.

Grace knew she should have backed off there and then but there was something mesmeric about his hazel eyes.

'It's pink tulle over silk,' she informed him.

'I thought as much,' he teased. 'The

colour goes well with your tan. Have you been away?'

'Only to the south of France.'

'I'm impressed. My family always go to Cornwall in a caravan for our holidays.'

Grace bit her lip realising how spoiled she sounded. 'I'm sure it's lovely.' She tried to make amends. 'I only said only because it was a business trip with my father.' She lapsed into silence aware she was making things worse.

'I hate wearing ties. Do you think anyone would mind if I undid it?' Daniel asked.

'You're not supposed to this early in the evening.'

'Rules are made to be broken, wouldn't you say?'

Grace shivered. She had never had such a grown up conversation. It was the headiest experience of her life. If only the other girls could see her now. She toyed with a tendril of her hair in what she hoped was a sophisticated manner.

'I know we've only just met and all that,' Daniel began.

'Yes?' Grace asked in a shaky voice.

'But I think you're beautiful.'

'Do you?' she squeaked.

'Would you let me kiss you?' he asked.

'Why?'

'As a reward for rescuing you tonight. I mean, if I hadn't been here you might have plunged into the lake.'

The kiss when it came was incredibly gentle and closing her eyes, Grace gave herself up to the experience.

'What exactly do you think you're doing?' Melissa Harper's voice was like a whiplash cracking between them.

Grace gasped and would have wriggled away from Daniel, but he did not move.

'Hello, Melissa. I'm comforting Grace. She's had a nasty experience.'

'You vicious snake.' Melissa sounded a bit like a snake herself as she hissed at Grace. 'You've done nothing but cause trouble this evening.'

'I tried to apologise, but you turned your back on me.'

'So you thought you'd get your revenge by kissing my date, did you?'

'What? No. I didn't know you knew each other. I had no idea.'

So Daniel was the fiancé Melissa had boasted about? She couldn't look at him. She couldn't look at either of them.

'Sorry,' she sobbed then gathering up her dress she ran across the lawn.

Soon after the night of the ball, the rest of her world came crashing down around her as her beloved father died. Sycamore House had to be sold and her life changed for ever.

The last Grace heard of Melissa was that she had moved out of the area and was now engaged to a successful businessman with interests all over the world.

She had never seen or heard from Daniel Stafford again — until today.

The sound of Foxy lapping up some water from the little bowl she had provided drew her attention back to the present. She wondered briefly why

Daniel's dog had been running loose and where he had been.

The telephone rang sharply.

'Fieldling Surgery, Grace speaking. How can I help you?' she asked.

'Hi there, Fieldling Surgery. It's Charlie Maxwell here.'

'Charlie,' she greeted her brother. 'When did you get back?'

'Last night. I would have called in at the post house, but I thought a late night visitor might spook the ladies. How are they, by the way?'

'Fine. How are you?'

'Much the same as usual. Hard up and looking for an injection of funds.'

'What happened to the job?'

'Things didn't turn out quite as I'd planned.'

'They never do.' It was a story Grace had heard many times before.

'Don't be like that, sis. Mum sends her love, by the way. So does Philippe.'

'I must visit them soon, but I've been so busy I haven't had time.'

'Fancy some lunch?' he asked.

'I can't,' Grace replied. 'There's a lot going on here at the moment. I can't leave.'

'Mr Vincent's a slave driver, you know that?'

'Not at all.'

'I'm sure you could take an hour out of your busy schedule to have a sandwich with me.'

'Not today.'

'Why not?'

'It's a long story.'

'Will it keep?' Charlie asked.

'Why don't you come round for supper tonight? Where are you staying?'

'On a friend's sofa. I suppose Amelia MacPherson wouldn't let me stay at the post house?'

'You suppose right,' Grace agreed, 'and it's not fair to ask her. She would probably say yes out of politeness and there really isn't room.'

'Thought you'd say that. By the way, I've heard a rumour someone new has moved into Sycamore House.'

'Daniel Stafford,' Grace replied.

'That name's familiar.'

'He used to be engaged to Melissa Harper.'

'Right,' Charlie agreed. 'Wasn't there some unpleasantness between the two of you?'

'It was a long time ago.' Grace tried to steer the conversation away from Daniel Stafford.

'Hold on.' Charlie wasn't to be diverted. 'It's all coming back to me now. She was the one whose engagement you broke up because she caught you kissing her Daniel in the rose garden or something, wasn't it?'

'It was down by the lake and I didn't know they were engaged.'

'Caused a bit of a stink at the time, didn't it?'

'Can we talk about something else?' Grace asked.

'Phew, I foresee fireworks should you meet up with him. Let me know if you need some help and I'll come to your aid. Mind you, my beautiful big sister has always been pretty good at looking after herself, hasn't she?'

'How long are you home for this time?' Grace didn't answer his question.

''Til I can get fixed up with some work. There's a man I need to see regarding a job crewing on his boat, but that's not until next week. I'll probably do a bit of temporary work down in the marina until then. I like to keep my tan topped up.'

'Do you need some money?'

'I always need money,' Charlie replied.

'How much this time?'

'I'll pay you back, I promise.'

Grace had heard that excuse many times before. Her younger brother had not adapted well to a life deprived of the luxuries they had grown up with. Project after project failed and he was constantly short of work and cash.

Their mother had met his debts until she married Philippe. Whilst the two men got on well, Philippe insisted Charlie find proper work and his allowance from his mother ceased on her re-marriage. From that day, Charlie had turned his attentions to his sister and his constant demands on her purse meant she was always short of money.

Grace loved her brother and he had a kind heart but there were times when she wished he would remember she had to work for her living, too, and that she wasn't a constant source of finance.

'We'll talk about it this evening,' she said. 'See you about seven?'

'Fine with me. I'll have to find someone else to treat me to lunch,' Charlie replied. 'I've just remembered something else,' he said. 'Wasn't Daniel Stafford training to be a vet?'

'Yes,' Grace said in a guarded reply.

'You'd better watch out he doesn't take over Mr Vincent's practice.'

'What makes you say that?' Grace asked. At times her brother was far too astute for comfort.

'Well, I wouldn't put much on your chances of staying in that cushy job of yours if he did take over.'

'I am a very good receptionist,' Grace retaliated. 'I work hard and I hardly ever have a day off.'

'Hey,' Charlie said, 'have I stumbled on the truth? Is that why Daniel has moved into Sycamore House? He really is taking over the surgery?'

'Yes.'

'That explains why you can't do lunch. Well, good luck.' There was laughter in Charlie's voice as he added, 'Perhaps you could try kissing him again if you want to keep your job.'

'I have no intention of kissing Daniel Stafford now or at any time in the future.'

'Calm down, sis. I didn't mean to upset you. See you later.' Charlie cut the call and Grace hung up.

The sound of a throat being cleared behind her made her jump.

'Sorry, I, er rang the bell, but I don't think it's working.'

She spun round.

'My goodness.' The man reeled at the sight of her bruised face. 'Have you just

49

gone six rounds with a heavyweight boxer?'

Foxy gave a bark of delight and leapt towards his master.

'D . . . Daniel,' Grace stuttered. 'How long have you been standing there?'

'Long enough to know you work hard, hardly ever take a day off and have absolutely no intention of kissing me again,' he replied with a devastating smile.

Family Woes

Grace pinned Mr Vincent's postcard onto the notice board in the middle of the advertisements for baby guinea pigs. Everyone would want to know how he and his wife were getting on and it would provide a good topic of conversation in the waiting room.

Grace was pleased she had won the argument over the notice board.

'We need to convey a more professional image,' Daniel insisted on his first day. 'I want a clean, efficient, stylish waiting room, not somewhere that looks as though a hurricane has hit it. That thing can go for a start.'

He pointed to the board.

'If it goes, so do I,' Grace retaliated, more than prepared to carry out her threat.

They glared at each other before Daniel came out with, 'If it wasn't for

51

that wretched clause in the contract Mr Vincent made me sign, you wouldn't have to resign. You wouldn't be here in the first place.'

Mr Vincent had insisted Grace should be allowed to stay in her job for at least two months after the change over. She and Daniel were now a month into the new arrangement and it wasn't going well.

'The clients like her and it helps to keep a sense of continuity,' he explained to a sceptical Daniel who had proposed ideas of a remote booking system via a central computer. 'We have always preferred personal contact and some of our older clients are not computer literate.'

Grace had been similarly appalled when she had learned of Daniel's plans.

'Who is Maisie?' Daniel strode over to read out one of the notices.

'Old Mrs Watts's budgerigar.'

'And why are its domestic arrangements of such importance they have to be so prominently displayed?'

'She downsized from her cottage to a warden controlled apartment and where she moved to they aren't allowed to keep caged birds, so she gave it to the school for their pets project. Mrs Watts pops in every now and then and the children leave little notes for her on the board explaining what they have been doing with Maisie and how she is getting on and helping them with their project.'

The look on Daniel's face would have made Grace laugh if she hadn't felt so strongly about the communication importance of the notice board.

'Can't Mrs Watts visit the school?'

'No, her legs are bad. She's a little deaf on the telephone too, so we do our bit for the community by posting on the board. Mrs Watts comes in here of a Friday morning with some cakes and we have coffee and catch up on the week's news.'

'All this socialising is going to have to stop,' Daniel insisted. 'We can't have half the village clogging up the waiting room, gossiping. This is a working surgery.'

'The work gets done as well and the surgery is a social hub of village life,' Grace insisted, wondering when the devil-may-care Daniel Stafford she remembered had turned into an unfeeling business machine.

He was twenty-six now and although the years had treated him kindly regarding looks, his character had changed. He wore business suits and seemed intent on maintaining targets. Grace couldn't see their relevance to the Fieldling practice, but she had expected change when Mr Vincent had retired and Daniel had more than lived up to that promise.

'No wonder Foxy ran out in front of my car,' her eyes were bright with indignation as she confronted Daniel, 'if you leave the poor dog alone all day.'

'What I do with my dog is my own business.'

'Why don't you bring him here? He's such an engaging little character. The patients would love him and I could keep an eye on him for you. That way he wouldn't get into more trouble.'

A fleeting expression of something like regret crossed Daniel's face as if he were remembering Grace's bruised face.

'I'm sorry about the accident, Grace,' he said with a trace of the old Daniel. 'I wish you would let me settle your garage bill and of course I will make amends for any other expenses you incurred.'

Grace shook her head. 'The garage said they wouldn't charge me if I let them advertise their services on our notice board for free so we did a deal and I'm not talking about money, I'm talking about letting a lonely little dog have some fun.'

'We are here to work, not to have fun.'

'Isn't it possible to occasionally combine the two?'

Grace was talking to his back as he headed for the office. Quelling the urge to stick her tongue out at him, she carried on addressing flyers announcing the change of management at the practice and stuffing them into envelopes.

The news had been met with varying degrees of welcome in Fieldling.

'I've known the Vincents all my life,' several regulars informed Grace, 'father and son. What do we want with some yuppy? He'll be full of posh ideas, all potted plants and all the fung shoo nonsense.'

'I think you mean feng shui,' Grace corrected Mr Barns as she strove to keep a straight face, 'and Mr Stafford hasn't mentioned anything about the décor.'

'He will,' Mr Barns prophesied darkly.

Privately Grace agreed with him. From the very first day nothing had been right, from the notice board to the higgledy piggledy collection of coffee mugs on the draining board in the kitchen.

'Doesn't any of the crockery match in this place?' he demanded.

'Mr Vincent didn't think it was important as long as we had a plentiful supply of coffee and biscuits.'

'No more biscuits,' Daniel insisted.

'What?'

'I see from the petty cash vouchers we got through ten packets last week.'

'Everyone wanted to know about you,' Grace tried to explain. 'The vicar's wife even bought you a cake.'

'I didn't get a slice.'

'Stop whinging,' Grace said before she remembered to whom she was talking. 'I did cut you a slice but you didn't eat it because you were out all day up at the farm attending to that sick calf.'

'Which meant I didn't have any lunch. A slice of home made cake would have been very welcome.'

'Well, I ate it. It would have been stale by the time you returned.' Grace seized her advantage. 'Now if the same thing should happen again you could raid the biscuit tin.'

A reluctant smile hovered on Daniel's lips and Grace detected a trace of the old Daniel, the one who had kissed her under the stars and comforted her in her distress and had the courage not to deny what he was doing when his fiancée confronted them.

'Take my calls,' he instructed her. 'I shall be busy doing figure work this morning.'

'Sure you don't want me to plug the telephone into the computer? Who knows, it might even make the tea if you ask it nicely?'

The look Daniel now cast in her direction was enough to convince Grace she had perhaps gone too far.

She mumbled an apology.

The telephone began to ring the moment Daniel closed the interconnecting office door and before Grace realised it the hands of the clock pointed to lunch-time. Mr Vincent always allowed her to have a break in the middle of the day as some evenings they worked late, but

Grace was reluctant to ask the same favour of Daniel.

Charlie had mentioned something about meeting up for lunch but as he hadn't firmed up and was notoriously unreliable when it came to dates, Grace decided to make do with some coffee and biscuits hoping Daniel would let her leave on time tonight.

It was Amelia MacPherson's bridge night. She and her sister liked to have an early supper and Grace always covered in the shop for them.

Often it didn't close before nine o'clock of an evening and it could be a very busy time with the office workers coming in to buy something to cook for their supper. Mr Vincent wouldn't have needed telling, but Daniel didn't really understand village life and the importance of the bridge club.

As the kettle boiled, Grace tried to remember what she did know about Daniel's background. Although he was from Sussex, he wasn't from their village. If he had been, the local network system would have been able to update her on all his background, but no-one seemed to know anything much about him.

One or two people thought his mother might have been a supply teacher who had stayed over for a whole term at the local infants' school because the regular teacher was sick and someone else had suggested his father had been an arable farmer, but they weren't too sure exactly where.

Grace nibbled on a biscuit. If Daniel did decide to dispense with her services she didn't know what she would do. There was her post office and general stores work, but the sisters couldn't afford to pay her well and sometimes when they forgot she didn't have the heart to remind them. They had come to her aid at a difficult time in her life when her friends in the village could be counted on the fingers of one hand.

Grace sighed. She poured hot water onto the coffee granules then went to answer the telephone as it began to ring again.

★ ★ ★

'I'm sorry, sis,' Charlie apologised as she thrust the letter under his nose.

'Do you know anything about this?' she demanded.

'You said I could borrow your car.'

'I didn't say you could park it in a prohibited zone.'

'I didn't know it was prohibited.'

'The bays outside the executive flats are designated parking areas and there are notices all over the place.'

'I realise that now.'

'This letter says it was there all day and as the car is registered in my name, I've got to pay the fine.'

'I'll pay you back,' Charlie said without much conviction.

The sun was streaming through the window of the local bistro. Two cappuccinos were on the table in front of them, but Grace wasn't in the mood for coffee.

'When?' she demanded.

'When I get a job.'

'Where have I heard that one before?' Grace raised her eyebrows.

'I mean it, sis. I will.'

'You do realise that not only did you infringe the local regulations, but you also parked in the doctor's bay?'

'I didn't, did I?' Charlie's open face was an expression of genuine regret.

'You did and he's not best pleased about it.'

'Want me to have a word with him?'

'Dr Malcolm?' Grace queried and watched the smile drain from Charlie's face. 'Exactly,' she said when the significance of the name had sunk in. 'Not even your charm would work on him.'

Dr Malcolm had been their mother's general practitioner and there had been a period in her life when Mrs Maxwell, as she then was and a martyr to her nerves, had taken to calling him out at all hours of the day and night.

In the end he had refused to treat her and quite unfairly blamed Charlie and Grace for their mother's behaviour.

Charlie had had a dalliance with the doctor's daughter earlier in the summer. It had been no more than a bit of fun to Charlie.

He was the sort of boy who was friendly with all the girls, but Eileen had taken their relationship more seriously. When she realised he was seeing other girls there had been a bit of a scene between them. Somehow or other Grace had got involved in the fall out and from that day Doctor Malcolm's family had not spoken to any of the Maxwells.

Grace didn't doubt the doctor would make full mileage out of the parking infringement and not dream of waiving the charges. She was dreading receiving the penalty fine. There were times when Charlie's thoughtlessness tested even her devoted sisterly love.

On Monday morning Grace's worst fears were confirmed. The doctor had gone to the local newspaper and insisted on a front page spread, citing the insensitivity of certain young people who ought to know better than to block his parking space.

'I could have been prevented from attending an emergency,' Doctor Malcolm was quoted as saying. 'The young lady concerned,' he didn't name Grace, but further down in the article was a picture of her car parked outside the post house. Everyone would recognise it as hers, 'just couldn't be bothered to park properly. It's time to make an example of this sort of thing. No-one is above the law.'

The authorities anxious not to upset the doctor had made an example and Grace received a stinging penalty notice in the post that had made her eyes water.

There was a copy of the newspaper on her desk when she arrived at work.

'What's this?' Daniel demanded pointing to the offending article.

'I'm sorry,' Grace began.

'This sort of thing is a slur on the practice.'

'It doesn't actually mention the

practice anywhere in the article.'

'It does on the social networking sites. It also mentions you by name and,' he paused, 'your past.'

'That was a long time ago.'

'That's as may be, but you can't keep things quiet these days.'

'Doctor Malcolm can go a bit over the top.'

'He has every right to on this occasion. Don't you realise your days of riding roughshod over everyone are over? You have to obey the rules like everyone else.'

'How dare you lecture me?' Grace slammed her bag down on the desk. 'I've done nothing but be reminded of my past nearly every day for five years.'

She could feel anger clogging the back of her throat. 'What happened to the family wasn't my fault, but I have been made to feel responsible. Do you know what it's like to find your safe existence come crashing down around you, not to mention the emotional trauma of losing a beloved parent, a father people start saying horrid things about?

'If it hadn't been for the likes of Mr Vincent and the MacPherson sisters I don't know what I would have done. They were gracious enough to give me a chance to prove I could change and I have.'

'How can you explain this then?'

Grace bit her lip. No way was she going to blame Charlie for what had happened, besides Daniel had been aching for an excuse to dismiss her and she had just presented him with a perfect one.

'I can't.' She shook her head.

'You know what this means?'

'You want me to leave so you can install your horrible machine with beeping lights and heaven knows what other attachments in my place.'

'That's not what I said.'

Grace snatched up her bag.

'Where are you going?' Daniel demanded.

Pig-headed pride had always been

Grace's worst vice. Since her family's downfall she had tried to overcome it with a moderate degree of success, but faced with Daniel's uncompromising demeanour she couldn't help herself from saying, 'You don't have to fire me. I resign and I wish you luck with your new age technology.'

'You can't walk out.'

'Try stopping me.' Grace's dramatic exit was somewhat marred when she tripped over the step, but ignoring Daniel's concerned, 'Are you all right?' she strode off in the direction of the park.

She wasn't sure where she was going or what she would do now but she knew she had to get as far away from Daniel Stafford as she possibly could.

A Welcome Break

The moment the aircraft landed at Nice, on the Côte d'Azur, Grace felt all the stress of the past month melt away. She only ever travelled light and clutching her compact hand luggage she was striding through the terminal towards the bus station moments after her arrival.

She inhaled the smell, an eclectic mixture of palm trees, lavender, garlic, floor polish and kerosene. It was always the same when she visited her mother and her new husband, Philippe, that peculiar smell unique to Nice, the playground of the rich and famous, but Philippe LeGrand was neither rich nor famous. He and Grace's mother ran a thriving bed and breakfast business on the outskirts of Nice.

The perched villages were originally built in the Middle Ages as a refuge during turbulent political times. Their lofty positions ensured uninterrupted views over the coast and the lower villages. Many still retained their original features — winding cobbled streets, elaborate town square fountains, religious buildings, some even boasted battlements and portcullises.

The first time Grace had visited her mother after her move to France she had been entranced by the romanticism of their château. The building was not as grand as the description implied. It was a working château, built in the eighteenth century by the son of a nobleman who needed a base for his family while he was away on his extensive travels.

Throughout the years it had suffered at the hands of history and for a while had fallen into disrepair. Then with a revival of interest in native craftworks and encouragement from the authorities to develop the site, Philippe had recognised the business opportunity of the area and purchased the crumbling château for a fraction of its market price.

With the revival of the craft centre, the village was subjected to a constant throng of visitors and advance booking was needed to ensure a room at Philippe's up-market bed and breakfast.

Grace would not have believed her mother could enjoy bed making, cleaning and preparing breakfast for their guests, but to her surprise, Teresa loved the excitement and constant challenge. She shopped in the local market for the fresh produce of the day and, as she was now fluent in the French language, bartered with the stallholders for the best deals.

These days her nerves no longer troubled her. Her complexion was Mediterranean tanned, her blonde hair glowed and Philippe, her husband of two years, adored her.

'Of course you must come and visit, darling.' Teresa had been delighted to receive Grace's telephone call. 'Bring some marmalade. Charlie meant to but as usual he forgot.'

She headed towards the airport bus

queue. Philippe had promised to meet her at the Gare Routière as he had some business to attend to in Nice. With buses leaving every twenty minutes Grace didn't have long to wait. The short ride into the centre gave her time to assemble her jumbled thoughts.

These days her mother's life in Fieldling was very far removed from that with Philippe, but Grace supposed she would need to know that Sycamore House had been sold and that the new owner, Daniel Stafford, had also taken over Mr Vincent's practice. An edited version of subsequent events would be the best choice, Grace decided.

When she had cooled down, Grace realised it hadn't been the wisest thing to do, storming out of the surgery, but there were only so many knocks her pride could take and Daniel had provided a knock too far.

The bus drew into the station. Grace spied Philippe on the pavement looking out for her.

'Yoo hoo!' She waved enthusiastically,

and the next moment she was scooped up in her stepfather's arms and subjected to a Gallic embrace, involving much kissing of cheeks and exclamations of delight.

'You are more beautiful than ever,' Philippe said, 'but you are recovering I think from the black eye?' he tutted. 'What have you been doing?'

'You should have seen me the day after it happened,' Grace laughed, 'and don't worry it was nothing serious,' she said anxious to dispel his concern, 'just a minor knock.'

'I am pleased to hear it. Teresa needs only the slightest excuse to worry. You know what your mother is like.'

'How is Mum?' Grace asked as the climbed into Philippe's battered 2 CV, the best sort of vehicle to drive along the twisting mountain roads, when oncoming lorries and buses were no respecters of expensive car paintwork.

'Very well. Last week we had some English ladies to stay, basket weavers, members of a guild and they were here to give a demonstration to their counterparts in the village. Your mother went along to translate for them and she had a very interesting time.'

'So business is good?' Grace asked.

'Extremely. We are coming into the holiday season and we are fully booked every week save this one, so you have chosen well. You and Teresa will have plenty of time to be together. I have insisted that she takes a rest. You know if I didn't stop her she would work twenty-four hours a day.'

Skirting the centre of Nice, Philippe took the narrow road leading up to their village. Once or twice Grace was forced to close her eyes as oncoming traffic forced them to go far closer to the edge than she would have liked.

'Nearly there,' Philippe said sensing Grace's discomfort. She had forgotten French driving habits and as they swung round bend after bend her head began to spin. 'Why don't you tell me about your love life? It might distract you from the sheer drop.'

'I don't have a love life,' Grace admitted.

Philippe was a typical Frenchman when it came to matters of the heart. He could not understand why at the age of twenty-three, Grace did not have a boyfriend.

'You have not broken any hearts?'

'Not one.'

'That is terrible. It should not be allowed. What are those cold Englishmen thinking of?'

'I don't really have time for much of a social life of any sort. I'm at the surgery all day then in the evenings I help the sisters out in the store.'

'Well, we shall see what we can do for you out here. Do you fancy, perhaps, an artist?'

'I don't think I'm much of a one for late nights,' Grace laughed. 'What I'm here for is to have a good time, do a bit of sight-seeing, eat some wonderful French food and enjoy an occasional glass of wine and play catch up with my mother. Do you realise it's been six months since I've seen her?'

'Is it that long?' Philippe looked surprised. 'Time goes so quickly. You know we had Charlie out for a visit a little while ago?'

'Yes, he forgot the marmalade.' Grace held up her shopping bag. 'I didn't.'

'Good girl,' Philippe nodded in approval. 'Our English guests like it and so do I. What was I saying?'

'Charlie?'

'Yes. Did he mention Odile?'

'I don't think so.'

'She is the daughter of a neighbour of ours and they had quite a thing going while he was out here. You must meet Odile. She's a very nice girl, about your age.'

'Don't tell me Charlie's fallen in love. He likes to play the field.'

'Not with Odile, I don't think. He said he was going home to earn some money then he was coming back to propose to her.'

'He said all that?' It was all Grace could do to contain her disbelief.

'Here we are.'

The remainder of the journey had passed quickly and without too many traumas. Philippe tooted his horn as they drew into the forecourt of the château. He circuited the fountain and came to a halt by the huge oak door and moments later it was flung open and her mother ran down the steps, arms outstretched.

'Darling.' She hugged her daughter. 'What have you been doing to yourself?'

'Hello, Mum,' Grace replied from the depths of her mother's embrace, 'good to see you too.'

'There are dark circles under your eyes and you're very pale. Don't you think so, Philippe?'

He kissed his wife on the cheek.

'Nothing a little good cooking and sunshine won't put right, cherie.' He held up Grace's bag. 'Is this all your luggage?'

'You know I travel light,' Grace replied.

'Then we will go shopping for some

new clothes.' Teresa clapped her hands. 'We are going to have such fun. I want to show you the recently discovered mosaics in the chapel. They are so pretty. There's a rumour they date back to Roman times.'

'Perhaps first we could all go inside?' Philippe suggested. 'Out of the sunshine?'

Teresa linked arms with both of them and the trio made their way into the cool interior of the château. Philippe went in search of some refreshment while Teresa and Grace made their way onto the patio that overlooked the coastal valley below them.

Grace settled down on one of the wicker chairs while her mother adjusted the sunshade.

'So, what's wrong?' she asked Grace.

'Why should anything be wrong?' Grace countered.

'A mother always knows,' Teresa smiled.

Philippe created a welcome diversion with a tray and two glasses and a jug of apricot juice.

'I'll leave you girls to gossip. It's so

lovely having you to stay. You'd be very welcome to live with us always if you like.'

His words caused a lump in her throat. 'Thank you, Philippe,' she replied in a hoarse voice. She watched Philippe go back into the main house before speaking again.

'Sycamore House has been sold.'

Teresa poured out some juice for them.

'I'm pleased to hear it. Perhaps we can now all move on?' Grace was relieved the news did not appear to upset her mother. 'You have heard about Charlie and Odile?' Teresa asked.

'Philippe mentioned a romance.'

Teresa nodded. 'It looks as though it could be serious. So all we need to do now is get you settled, don't we?'

'I've already had this conversation on the drive up with Philippe. There is no-one significant in my life at the moment.'

'That's because you work too hard.'

'I have to. Charlie . . . '

'Can look after himself. It took me a while to realise that granting him an allowance was not the way to make him stand on his own two feet.'

Grace hesitated, wondering whether or not to tell her mother about Dr Malcolm, then decided against it. There was no point in stirring up the past and it would do no good telling her that by cutting off Charlie's allowance she had transferred the problem to Grace.

'Mr Vincent has retired,' she began.

'Who has taken over?'

'The man who purchased Sycamore House. His name is Daniel Stafford.'

Grace held her breath. Would her mother remember?

After a short pause her mother asked, 'And he didn't want to keep you on?'

'We had a difference of opinion,' Grace admitted, knowing it would be useless trying to pull the wool over her mother's eyes, 'regarding business methods.'

'I see.' Teresa sipped some of her juice. 'And is this Daniel Stafford young?'

'Twenty-six.'

Teresa nodded. If she remembered the incident at the prom ball it seemed she wasn't going to mention it.

'What will you do about getting a new job?'

'I have my work at the post office to help me out.'

'Why don't you take up Philippe's offer of work here? Your French is adequate and after a few months you would be fluent.'

'I have to make my own way, Mum,' Grace insisted, 'much as I'd like to live the life of sun, sea and sand.'

'At times you are so very like your father,' she sighed. 'I'm sure things would have worked out differently if he hadn't fallen ill. He always wanted to do the best by everyone, but in the end he exhausted himself. Don't make the same mistake, my darling.'

'I won't,' Grace promised.

She was beginning to feel hot in her long sleeved shirt and trousers.

'Could we go clothes shopping tomorrow?' she asked, 'I only brought the bare essentials with me.'

'My treat,' Teresa insisted, 'as you won't let me do anything else for you. There's a divine new boutique opened in the next village, and I think we need to get your hair styled and highlighted and your nails done, of course.'

Teresa was in her element and moments later the pair of them were happily discussing plans for their holiday.

A Change In Charlie

Teresa was as good as her word and the following week she and Grace hit the boutiques and the open-air market.

'You must stop buying me things,' Grace protested when her mother draped a pale-blue cobweb shawl around her shoulders.

'Darling, it is perfect for the summer evenings and the colour exactly matches your eyes. *Combien*? How much?' she asked the stallholder then proceeded to engage in lively debate as she beat him down to a friendlier price.

As cars were not allowed through the cobbled streets, they walked happily from one shop to another. Teresa treated herself to a new sun hat in one of the small boutiques tucked down a side turning.

'This would look good on Mademoiselle.' The sales lady produced a plain white shift dress.

Before Grace could protest further she was bundled into a back room. The simple dress slid over her shoulders. She hardly recognised the sleek sophisticate looking back at her in the mirror.

'You have to have it,' her mother endorsed the assistant's sales patter.

'Where would I go in a dress like this?'

'Out to dinner,' the assistant said, 'an evening with friends? It is a perfect piece for your capsule wardrobe.'

'A birthday present, I insist.' Teresa began searching in her bag for her credit card, 'to go with your new blue shawl.'

Sheets of tissue paper were already being produced and Grace was hustled back into the changing room and the dress whipped off her before she could talk her mother into changing her mind.

Clutching a large dress box they emerged into the sunlit street.

'Have you had a good day?' Teresa asked as they headed out of the village towards the small car park.

'Wonderful,' Grace squeezed her mother's arm. 'You know how to spoil a girl.'

'I like spoiling you. Besides,' she added looking unnaturally serious, 'I realise how hard things were for you after your father died.'

'It wasn't your fault, Mum,' Grace began to protest.

'I wasn't much use to you, was I? You had to carry the family and it can't have been easy. No,' she held up a hand, 'let me have my say, then we won't mention it again. I want you to know how proud I am of you. You didn't fall by the wayside like Charlie and me. You went out and got yourself a job and somewhere to live.'

'So did you.'

'That was pure chance. If Philippe hadn't bumped into me on the pavement and seen I was crying and taken pity on me, I would still be a pathetic wreck.' Her mouth softened into a smile. 'Do you know he thought I had tears in my eyes because he had hurt me when he bumped into me?

'I didn't let on of course that it had been that horrid Dr Malcolm who had upset me. There are some things a girl should keep to herself. Anyway with true French gallantry Philippe scooped me up, bought me a glass of wine in the middle of the day, would you believe, and treated me to lunch. The next thing I knew he had dried my tears and invited me over to France. Talk about a whirlwind romance.'

'And you've never looked back?'

'And you are not to spill the beans about the true reason for my tears because Philippe still doesn't know.'

'Would I?'

'No, you wouldn't and I know it will remain our secret. One more thing, before the subject is closed. It was Daniel Stafford who caused all that unpleasantness with Melissa Harper, wasn't it?'

'You remembered his name?'

'I didn't like to say anything when it happened because I know how upset you were, but I had Melissa's wretched mother on the telephone accusing you of all sorts of things. I know I was a bit flaky at the time but I wasn't putting up with that. I'm not ashamed to admit we had things out and when I'm riled, well, I speak my mind.'

'Mum, you are a star. I owe you one.'

'That's what I'm trying to say. My advice is you are not to stand any more nonsense from Daniel Stafford. He has already disrupted your life once and if he should upset you again, give him what for and remember if you need reinforcements, I'm on your side.'

'Well, I'm glad you got that off your chest.' Grace kissed her mother's cheek. 'With you and Charlie both offering to fight my corner, how can I lose?'

They completed the journey back to the château without any major incidents, apart from the dress box sliding to and fro across the back seat.

'I thought Philippe said you had no bookings for this week,' Grace said as they drew into the forecourt as a taxi

86

was drawing out.

'We haven't and if anyone calls I told him to say we weren't open. I wanted some quality time with you. Who on earth can it be?'

'Hello, girls,' a friendly voice called across to them.

'My heavens.' Teresa was out of the car almost before Grace had stopped the engine and running for all she was worth towards their unexpected visitor.

The sight of her six-foot tall brother being hugged by their diminutive mother was too much for Grace. She burst into laughter. Charlie joined in and soon the three of them were convulsed. Philippe emerged from the château to see what all the noise was about.

'Mon Dieu, what is going on?' he demanded. 'Have we been invaded?'

His greeting matched that of his wife as he spied Charlie.

Philippe had no children of his own and had always treated both Grace and Charlie as his offspring and soon the two men were male bonding, discussing football results and hotly debating the legality of the winning goal at the previous week's international between France and England.

'Isn't it lovely?' Teresa said as they made their way inside. 'Both my children here with me. I couldn't be happier. I know, let's invite a few friends round for drinks tomorrow. Philippe, you could do one of your special fish platters. What do you think?'

'An excellent idea,' he called over his shoulder.

'Charlie,' Teresa's eyes twinkled with mischief, 'I'm sure you would like to see Odile again? She was asking about you only the other day.'

Grace watched her brother's face turn a colourful shade of pink.

'You haven't been saying anything, have you?' he demanded.

'About what?' Teresa looked deceptively innocent.

'Me, my past, you know.'

'Old girlfriends you mean? Darling, I

don't think I could list them even if I tried and don't worry, I praised you to the skies. I think Odile is a lovely girl and I wouldn't want to upset her. Now why don't you and Grace sit on the terrace while Philippe and I prepare some salad and nibbles?'

'I got all your messages, eventually,' Charlie said as they sat down outside. 'What exactly happened between you and Daniel? Amelia MacPherson said he blamed you for parking in the doctor's space.'

'That about sums it up,' Grace admitted. 'Mum doesn't know anything about the doctor, by they way. I didn't think it wise to bring up his name.'

'Understand,' Charlie agreed, 'but it is true? Daniel sacked you because of me?'

'He didn't actually sack me. I stormed out.'

'What did you do that for?' Charlie demanded.

'We hadn't been getting on that well.'

'What went wrong between you?'

'Silly things like him wanting to get rid of the notice board in the surgery.'

'He can't do that.'

'That's what I told him, but well, there were other things. Mr Vincent had insisted Daniel keep me on for at least two months during the takeover period, but it was obvious he didn't want me. He suggested an automated answering system and if he had to have a receptionist well probably someone a little more glamorous who didn't question all his new practices.'

'That's about the most stupid thing I've heard in my life.'

'Stupid or not, it's what he wants.'

'You virtually ran the surgery for Mr Vincent. Doesn't Daniel realise that?'

'I've no idea, but I wasn't going to give him the satisfaction of dismissing me, so I dismissed myself and caught the first flight down here for a holiday.'

'Do you want me to explain to Daniel that what happened was my fault not yours?'

'No.' Grace shook her head firmly.

'Least said, soonest mended.'

'Then what are you going to do? Are you going to stay here and take up Philippe's offer of a job?'

'I love being here, but it's their life, not mine. I help out, of course, when I'm needed, but I have to go back to Fieldling. I couldn't desert Amelia and Beattie. They rely on me and I've got my work at the post office to tide me over. I could do a few more hours for them.'

'It's not much of a life for you,' Charlie protested. 'You could be out sunbathing every day. Dining on luxury yachts, mixing with the jet set.'

Grace shuddered. 'That sort of thing is not for me any more.'

'You're thinking of Dad, aren't you?' Charlie said in a soft voice.

'To be honest, Charlie, I think when our lifestyle changed, it was a wake up call. Now I'm much happier trudging around the countryside with proper people in all sorts of weather, getting my boots dirty, enjoying the simpler things of life.'

'Well, when you start job hunting don't undersell yourself,' Charlie insisted, 'and if you ever want me to take up my offer to sort out Daniel Stafford, just let me know.'

Grace smiled at her brother. 'Mum offered the same service this afternoon.'

'We could always rope Philippe in, too, if you like. I'm sure he would be more than ready to join in. Daniel wouldn't stand a chance if we marched en masse to the surgery. I can see us now waving banners aloft like something out of the French Revolution.'

'What is all this laughter about?' Teresa enquired as she emerged on to the terrace.

Charlie leapt to his feet to relieve his mother of the tray of drinks she was carrying.

'We were talking about Grace going for long country walks in wellies and a wax jacket,' Charlie said with a wink at Grace.

'While you, my darling, are happy to indulge in the high life. Have you had any more thoughts about your water sports business?'

'I have, actually. I think I might give it a go. What do you think?'

'It would be a lot of hard work and you would need a good business plan.' Philippe appeared behind his wife, carrying a plate of tempting looking canapés. 'If you like I can get you some introductions.'

'That would be great, Philippe. So it's all right if I stay for a while?'

'You'll need to earn your keep,' Philippe said. 'That's only fair.'

'What change sheets, things like that?' Charlie now looked appalled.

'If your mother needs help with the housework, then yes, although I was thinking more along the lines of maintenance.'

'I could manage to change a few light bulbs. I suppose.' Charlie glanced at his watch. 'What time is supper?'

'You're not going out? You've only just arrived,' Grace protested.

'Why don't you invite Odile to join

us for supper?' Teresa asked. 'That way you could introduce her to Grace. I was going to suggest we visit her anyway, Charlie, even if you hadn't arrived.'

'Sure you don't mind her gate-crashing a family evening, Philippe?'

'She would be more than welcome and we have plenty of food. Ask her over and we'll discuss details for tomorrow's party. We could do a barbecue, perhaps, to go with the fish.'

'Good idea.' Charlie leapt to his feet, in his haste almost knocking over the drinks table. 'I won't be long.'

He kissed his mother and shook hands with Philippe.

'Great to be back here,' he said.

'If Charlie's plans come to fruition,' Teresa watched her son as he strode off down the drive, 'Odile will quite soon be part of the family anyway.'

'I've never known him behave like this with any of his other girlfriends,' Grace admitted with an indulgent smile. 'Who would have believed it? My little brother in love.'

'All we need to do now,' Philippe said, 'is to get you sorted out. Then both our children will be happy won't they, Teresa?'

The warmth Grace felt as Philippe referred to her as his child, was slightly chilled by the thought that should he ever meet up with Daniel Stafford, he might think he would make a perfect future partner in life for Grace.

'I'm happy as I am now,' she insisted. 'One romance in the family is quite enough to be going on with for the time being.'

'Anything you say, my darling,' Philippe smiled at her, 'but I should warn you, I don't do defeat.'

'Exactly what fillings are in these delicious-looking nibbles, Philippe?' Teresa asked passing the plate to Grace.

'In other words subject closed,' Grace said with a smile, adding, 'Mum's right. These are fantastic, Philippe.' Her cheeks bulged as she savoured her canapé.

'You will stay on here until your birthday, won't you, now Charlie has arrived?' Teresa insisted.

'We must celebrate with a cake and candles,' Philippe said.

'I'd rather not remember exactly how old I am,' Grace laughed.

'It's so lovely everyone being together. It doesn't happen very often. Indulge us,' Teresa pleaded.

'I'd love to have one of Philippe's special cakes for my birthday,' Grace gave in. 'I'll even let you sing to me if you like.'

'Charlie's always out of tune,' Philippe complained. 'You'll have to shut him up, Teresa.'

'There's Charlie and Odile now,' Teresa called out. 'Lovely to see you, cherie.' Teresa rose to her feet and kissed Odile. 'Come and meet my daughter, Grace.'

Grace hastily swallowed her canapé, wiped her fingers then looked up into the face of the most stunningly beautiful girl she had seen in her life.

An Offer From Daniel

'Go and have a good time,' Grace insisted. 'You and your sister need a break.'

'It has been such a long time since we've seen our old school friend and Devon is a lovely part of the world,' Amelia explained.

'Especially at this time of the year,' Grace agreed. 'I'll look after the shop. There's no need to worry about a thing. You deserve a holiday.'

'You are a good girl.' Amelia patted her hand. 'I'll telephone my friend now and tell her to expect us at the weekend.'

The back door to the kitchen was open and the garden was alive with the sounds of early summer. Grace had been back from France for a week now and her tan was beginning to fade. So far she hadn't caught a glimpse of

Daniel in the village, but Amelia MacPherson had told her that one or two of Mr Vincent's regulars had taken to catching the bus into the neighbouring town and visiting the vet there.

'The atmosphere isn't the same I've been told and everyone was most upset to discover he had fired you.'

'I left of my own free will.' Grace had been anxious to set the record straight. She didn't want Daniel accusing her of spreading unfounded rumours to blacken his name.

'I'm afraid the villagers don't believe that one,' Amelia coughed apologetically, 'and it's no good trying to convince them otherwise.'

Grace poured boiling water into the teapot then set out the cups and saucers. Although she would die rather than admit it, she was missing the buzz of the surgery and Mrs Watts's Friday treat of cream cakes. She hoped the school had found a way of keeping her in touch with her budgerigar.

In the past Grace had been accused

of letting her heart rule her head and this time she knew she was guilty. She shouldn't have walked out on Daniel without giving proper notice.

It was a totally unprofessional way to behave and not something she was proud of. Her behaviour would, she suspected, also jeopardise her search for another job.

'It's all arranged.' Amelia bustled back into the kitchen. 'We're catching the early morning train on Saturday.'

'I'll run you to the station,' Grace offered.

'That's very kind of you, dear.' Amelia opened the biscuit tin. 'Now we have a moment to ourselves, you must tell me all about your little break in France. How is your mother?'

After Grace had updated her on events at the château, including an in depth character sketch of Odile, whom Grace had discovered was one of the nicest people on the planet, it was time for her afternoon stint in the shop.

A customer was waiting on the

pavement as Grace unlocked the door.

'I didn't realise you closed for lunch.' The young woman swept in, bringing with her a waft of eye watering perfume. It was all Grace could do not to cough.

'We stay open all day Thursday through to Saturday and we are open on Sundays too.'

Grace's explanation was swept aside in a gesture of irritation.

'Can this go first class please? It's extremely important and is needed urgently by tomorrow morning.'

Grace settled down the other side of the security grill and weighed the packet on the scales all the while conscious of the customer's impatient drumming of her fingers.

As Grace did her calculations she sneaked a look at her out of the corner of her eye. The tawny hair had been professionally highlighted and the make up expertly applied, but there was no mistaking the high cheekbones or the unusual almond shaped violet eyes.

'There you are,' she said as she attached the postage to the package, 'all done.'

A frown marred the woman's smooth forehead.

'It's Grace Maxwell, isn't it?'

'Yes.' She smiled nervously. 'Hello, Melissa.'

There was no answering smile. She hoped Melissa wasn't going to make a scene. Her mother, Mrs Harper, had said all that had to be said five years ago.

'How are you?' Grace looked at the manicured nails and ringless fingers. She was sure she'd heard that Melissa was engaged to a businessman.

'I'm doing very well, thank you.' She picked an imaginary piece of cotton off her elegant black polo necked sweater as she looked around the cramped shop that sold everything from fresh fruit to talcum powder.

'I can't say the same about you. Working in a shop?' Melissa could barely keep the disbelief out of her voice. Her eyes lingered on Grace's serviceable uniform of T-shirt and jeans that were sporting a stain from where she'd spilt some washing up liquid down them. 'You have gone down in the world.'

'I'm happy,' Grace replied.

'Where are you living these days?'

'Above the store. You'd be surprised how much room there is in the post house.'

The plucked eyebrows rose several inches. 'Weren't you going to find yourself a rich man and get married?'

'Weren't you?' Grace retaliated then wished she hadn't. Bickering with Melissa would get her nowhere. It was difficult to believe they had once been such close friends.

Melissa tossed back her head. 'My fiancé and I decided to go our separate ways,' she admitted and Grace glimpsed the first chink in her old friend's armour.

'I'm sorry,' she said and meant it.

'There's no need to be,' Melissa

replied. 'These days I feel much more fulfilled. I'm my own person now.'

'What do you do?'

'I run a mobile beauty business — organic hair products, nail products, facials, vitamin supplements, all that sort of thing, for the busy woman of today. I do makeovers too. My order book is bulging.'

'I'm impressed,' Grace said. 'And are you visiting?'

'I've moved in with my sister. It's a temporary arrangement,' she explained, 'until I can get myself sorted out. I need a permanent base in the area and I'm currently viewing properties. It's a buyers' market so I'm not rushing into anything. Fieldling is on my list of possibles so I expect we'll bump into each other occasionally.'

Grace was wondering whether or not to suggest they meet up for a drink when the shop doorbell pinged. Her heart plummeted as Daniel Stafford walked into the store.

'Good heavens,' Melissa greeted him,

'what a day for meeting up with old friends.'

She kissed Daniel on both cheeks and gazed rapturously into his hazel eyes.

'You haven't changed a bit. You do remember me, don't you?' she asked when he didn't immediately respond to her greeting.

'Of course,' his voice sounded strained, 'Melissa. I haven't seen you in ages.'

Grace remembered the last time the three of them had been together and wondered what sort of conversation the other two had had down by the lake on prom night after she'd rushed off into the darkness, every part of her body aflame with embarrassment.

'How absolutely lovely to see you again. I didn't realise you were back in this part of the world. What are you doing here?'

'I'm the new vet.'

'Really?' Melissa arched an eyebrow. 'We must get together some time.' She began searching in the pockets of her designer handbag. 'Here is my mobile number. I'm staying with my sister. You remember her?'

'Yes of course,' Daniel replied automatically.

'Where are you living now?' Melissa asked.

'Sycamore House.'

Melissa's light laugh was like ice down Grace's spine. Neither of them had acknowledged her presence and she was beginning to feel as though she didn't exist. She wondered briefly if they would notice if she crept out of the back of the shop and left them to get on with their reunion without her.

'I always loved that house. I've spent many happy hours there playing tennis with Charlie Maxwell,' she paused, 'and Grace of course.'

Grace felt Daniel's hazel eyes flick in her direction.

'Hello, Daniel,' she greeted him.

'I see you're back from your holiday,' he looked past Melissa to where Grace was seated.

'You've been away?' Melissa elbowed her way back into the conversation.

'To visit my mother in France.'

'I heard that she married a Frenchman. So she got over her health problems?' Melissa put a hand to her mouth. 'Perhaps I shouldn't mention them. My mother had a bit of a tough time after my father died, but she pulled herself together. She lives in a villa in Menorca these days. I'm always flying out to visit her. Daniel,' she put a hand on his arm, 'we really must get together. I won't take no for an answer. This evening, perhaps?' she suggested.

'I have plans for this evening,' he replied.

'No matter. I'm incredibly busy, too,' Melissa gathered up her receipt for her parcel and flashed him a dazzling smile. 'Keep in touch.'

Without a further look at Grace she swept out of the store.

For a moment neither Grace nor Daniel spoke. Aware she was breathing heavily, Grace took a few moments out

106

to calm down. She stood up and came out from behind the security grill.

'Can I do anything for you?' she asked.

'I just wanted to check you really were back. One of the patients reported seeing you drive through the village yesterday morning.'

'As you heard I've been to visit my mother.'

Daniel nodded. 'You forgot these.'

He produced her employment documents and passed them over. 'You'll need them when you apply for another job.'

Any faint hope Grace had nursed that he had come to offer her old job back died.

'Thank you,' she said. 'How are things at the surgery?'

'I've implemented several new practices.'

'Including getting rid of the notice board?' Grace couldn't resist asking.

A reluctant smile twitched Daniel's lips. 'Actually, it stayed. There was almost a riot when I had it moved so I had it brought back,' he admitted.

'I'm pleased to hear it.'

'I have stopped Mrs Watts descending on me with a box of cream cakes of a Friday. I explained I didn't have time to chat to her and that she would be better off visiting the school in person.'

'She can't get there,' Grace began to explain.

'That's why I arranged for a car to pick her up every Friday and take her. She's led a very interesting life, apparently, and she is helping the children with their history project. She is really enjoying the challenge and experience of working with the youngsters, so winners all round, wouldn't you say?'

Grace blinked up at Daniel and wished she didn't find him so attractive. It almost choked her to admit it was a good idea.

'Have you got a new receptionist or have you gone fully automatic?'

'Another idea I realised wasn't quite

right,' Daniel's rueful smile softened his face. 'I'm conducting interviews later in the week,' he said.

'Good.' Grace nodded, determined not to succumb to his charm. 'Well, if there's nothing else?'

The shop had now attracted several more customers most of whom were pretending not to listen to their conversation.

'I was wondering if perhaps you'd like to come out for a meal tonight?'

'I beg your pardon?' Grace nearly dropped the change she was handing over to one of the customers as she rang up the purchase. 'Did you say tonight?'

'Yes. If you're busy of course I understand.'

'I thought you told Melissa you were busy.'

'I told her I had plans and my plans are to invite you out.'

'Well, er,' totally wrong footed Grace blinked back at him. 'I don't finish here until about seven-thirty.'

'That's fine. I've got mountains of paperwork to catch up. I'll call for you around eight, shall I?'

By now Grace was blushing furiously as Daniel excused himself for delaying the queue of inquisitive shoppers. Grace knew the news of their date would be round the village in seconds. She tried to smile at her next customer. It would have to be the village busybody she thought as she rang up her purchases.

'Thank you, dear,' the customer replied, adding, 'so glad you and Daniel are back together, but if I were you I'd keep an eye on that Melissa Harper. She's out to get him.'

Grace's smile grew even more strained as the queue began to discuss the real reason behind Melissa's return. She tried not to listen, but the general consensus of opinion was her engagement had failed because she was too pushy.

As Grace worked through the afternoon her thoughts were in turmoil. Why had Daniel asked her out? There had to be a reason. It obviously wasn't to offer her old job back. Surely it hadn't been a ruse merely to deter Melissa?

'I'll finish up here, dear,' Amelia offered as the early evening custom began to drift off. 'Why don't you go and have a nice bath to relax you before you get ready for your date with Daniel?'

'How did you know about that?' Grace asked.

She knew the village information system matched most sophisticated global technology but she hadn't realised it was quite so up to speed.

Grace mounted the stairs. The dress her mother had bought her in the French boutique would boost her confidence.

'It Was Nothing Serious'

The country club had changed hands several times since the night of the prom ball and it now boasted a spa and fitness centre as well as a much-acclaimed restaurant.

All the same, Grace had been surprised when Daniel had chosen it for their night out. She remembered the young girl she had been when she had forced her mother to drive her to the ball and how all their lives, hers, Melissa's and Daniel's, had changed since.

Grace glanced sideways at Daniel. If he was remembering their encounter here the expression on his face was giving nothing away.

Daniel had been a little early for their date and Amelia had greeted him at the door.

'Grace works so hard,' she explained

with a sweet smile, 'I had to drag her out of the shop and I'm afraid she isn't quite ready, but do come in. You haven't met my sister, Mrs Bishop? Beattie, Mr Stafford is the new vet. You remember Grace used to work for him until recently?'

Overhearing every word as she expected was Amelia MacPherson's intention, Grace hid a smile. Amelia had indeed insisted she leave the shop, but Grace had had plenty of time to get ready, as they both well knew.

Grace brushed her hair smiling to herself. For an unmarried lady Amelia certainly knew the rules of the dating game and as she had told Daniel Grace wasn't quite ready, Grace didn't see the need to go downstairs just yet.

She suspected Daniel was probably feeling most uncomfortable in the over heated lounge. When the mood was on them, Amelia and her sister went for plain speaking and they were most likely giving him a hard time.

Grace inspected her image in the

mirror. She decided the white shift dress, brightened up by the blue shawl was a perfect choice for the evening. Although the dress was new she felt comfortable wearing it. The delicate fabric looked good against her still lightly tanned skin.

She took a few deep breaths to calm her racing pulse. It was unlike her to suffer from nerves and she didn't know why they were affecting her tonight. Perhaps it was the shock of seeing Melissa again after so many years, then Daniel following her into the shop. It has brought the past racing back to meet her. A past she had desperately tried to throw off.

★　★　★

As they approached the clubhouse a valet opened Grace's door, then taking Daniel's keys drove the car into a suitable parking space overlooking the lake.

'Are those shoes up to a stroll before

dinner?' Daniel asked looking at Grace's sandals.

'As long as the management don't mind heels on their lawns?'

'That's perfectly all right, madam,' the valet replied, returning with Daniel's keys. 'I'll tell the restaurant manager you are here. Have a good walk.'

The evening was pleasantly cool. A fresh breeze fanned Grace's face as they strolled across the grass.

'Foxy sends his love, by the way,' Daniel said, taking her arm to guide her away from a rabbit hole.

'It was lucky it was only my car he ran in front of,' Grace replied. 'Some people drive far too fast down those country lanes.'

'I hope you didn't suffer any after effects?' Daniel's eyes searched her face. 'Your bump seems to have gone down.'

'You saw me at my worst,' Grace smiled.

'No headaches, nothing like that?'

'Nothing at all. You can rest easy.'

They walked with measured steps towards the lake.

'I had no idea Melissa was in the area, did you?' Grace asked to break the silence between them.

'No,' Daniel replied.

'I am sorry I split you up that night,' Grace said. 'No,' she stopped Daniel as he tried to speak. 'Let me get it off my chest. I was in a bad mood because Melissa had sprung it on me that she was engaged. We were supposed to be best friends and she had never said a word.

'My father had gone to all the fuss of ordering a limo and I thought she had spoiled the evening. I'm afraid in those days I was very spoilt and rather immature. Anyway, I threw a strop and, well, you know the rest of the story. When I poured my heart out to you, I had no idea she was actually engaged to you.'

'She wasn't.'

'I wasn't bent on some sort of revenge trip — what did you say?' Grace gasped.

'Steady.' Daniel caught her arm again

as Grace lost her footing for the second time.

'What do you mean Melissa wasn't engaged to you?' she asked.

'That's what I was trying to tell you. We'd been out a couple of times, but it was nothing serious and to be honest I was trying to cool things between us. Melissa was reading more into the relationship than I was and I wanted to break things off before anyone got hurt. I had no idea she was going round telling people we were engaged until you came out with it the night of the prom ball.

'I wanted to explain things at the time, but after all that business with your father, well,' Daniel paused, 'I decided the best thing I could do would be to get out of your life. Everyone had enough problems on their plates.'

'The past five years haven't been easy,' Grace admitted, 'I still have the occasional bad day, but I'm getting there.'

They had now reached the lake. As

they stood looking across the expanse of water, Grace hoped Daniel hadn't asked her down here again to kiss her. A tiny part of her wondered if he had seen Melissa approaching that night, and arranged the embrace in order to engineer a showdown with her. She shivered involuntarily as she remembered the undignified scene that followed.

'It's getting chilly.' Daniel noticed her shiver. 'Would you like to go in now? I expect you're hungry, too.'

Grace's lunch had only been the tea and biscuits she'd shared with Amelia before it had been time to open up the shop and she now realised her stomach felt very empty indeed.

'I think my shawl is better suited for the Mediterranean climate,' she agreed as she drew it around her shoulders.

They turned round and began to amble back towards the house.

'When did you realise I was Mr Vincent's receptionist?' Grace asked.

'Not until we were at a late stage in the negotiations,' Daniel replied. 'Our discussions were all very informal to begin with and we didn't go into details at first.'

They had now reached the main steps and a valet hurried down to meet them and to guide them towards the bright lights of the restaurant.

'I'll just pop to the ladies' and fix my lipstick, Daniel.'

'OK, I'll see you at the table.'

A few moments later she made her way back towards the dining room. It was bright and well lit and the picture windows created an airy atmosphere. The views swept down over the lawns that were now discreetly lit up.

In her other life she would have enjoyed being in this sort of environment. Now she wasn't so sure. Above the tinkling of glasses and the discreet murmur of conversation, she couldn't help feeling slightly out of place.

'Madam.' A waiter appeared at her side. 'If you'll follow me?'

Her heels tapped across the coconut matting as she walked across the floor.

Several male heads turned in her direction. One or two people smiled and acknowledged Grace. She hoped they were not remembering her family's scandalous past.

Daniel she saw was sitting at one of the bay window tables. He wasn't alone. By his side, laughing at his every utterance and seated far closer than could be comfortable was Melissa Harper.

An Awkward Date

Melissa's companion was the only one of the little group to get to his feet as Grace approached the table.

'Grace?' He greeted her with a friendly smile and outstretched arms.

'Jason.' She recognised one of Charlie's surfing friends. 'How lovely to see you.'

They kissed on the cheek as Jason gave her a friendly hug, and it was Jason who arranged a seat for her and saw her comfortably settled at the table. Melissa had pinioned Daniel into a corner. He was unable to move and Grace suspected that had been Melissa's intention.

She smiled across at them.

'Hello, Melissa. Fancy seeing you again so soon.'

'You should have told me,' Melissa wagged a finger at Daniel, 'that your plans for the evening were dinner with Grace.'

Grace opened her mouth to explain, but she wasn't given a chance to speak. Still ignoring her, Melissa carried on. 'We could have made up a foursome. As it is, you don't mind if we join you now, do you?' she asked Daniel.

Jason nudged Grace and raised an eyebrow at her. 'Do you?' he asked in a soft voice, adding in an even quieter tone, 'I can easily get you out of it if you and Daniel would rather be alone.'

Grace shook her head.

'You haven't interrupted a hot date and we're not an item,' Grace whispered back to Jason, 'and I want to hear all that you've been up to since we last met.'

The thought crossed her mind that perhaps the story Daniel had spun her down by the lake wasn't entirely true and that he was more involved with Melissa than he had let on. Grace tightened her lips. If that was the game he was playing she wasn't being set up for a second time.

'Daniel needs to get his eyesight tested then,' Jason smiled.

'Sorry?' Grace returned her attention to him.

'You look ravishing.'

She blushed at the enthusiasm with which Jason delivered his compliment.

'It's nice of you to say so,' she smiled.

'And you're absolutely sure you don't want me to separate Daniel and Melissa?'

'Only if you're on a hot date with Melissa?'

The horrified expression on Jason's face brought a smile to Grace's lips.

'She phoned me up out of the blue and somehow I found I had been talked into coming here tonight. To be honest I was dreading the prospect of an evening in her company, but I didn't know how to get out of it without sounding ungallant. Actually, I'd rather catch up on old times with you. That's a great dress you're wearing by the way.'

'You like it?' Grace smiled back into

his friendly face. It had been so long since anyone had complimented Grace on her appearance she had almost forgotten what it felt like. 'Thank you. It was a birthday present from my mother.'

'She lives in France now, doesn't she?'

'I've just been to visit her. Charlie was there.'

'I haven't seen him for ages. How is the old sea dog?'

Soon she and Jason were deep in conversation reminiscing about the old times.

'Poor old Charlie nearly drowned,' Jason laughed as he finished a story about the first ever lesson Charlie gave a novice surfer. 'His pupil was all arms and legs and the lifeguard didn't realise what was going on until she had dragged him down for the third time. Of course, our lot didn't help. We were laughing so much no-one realised he could have been in difficulty. Those were the days.'

'Sorry,' Grace looked up into the hovering waiter's face. 'I didn't realise you were ready to take our order.'

'That's quite all right, madam,' he smiled back at her. Not all patrons were so considerate and he appreciated the gesture. 'Will your friends be joining you, sir,' he asked Jason.

'Actually I made the booking,' Daniel cut in from the far end of the table, 'for two.'

'Silly me. I never thought to ask Grace. You don't mind if we join you, do you?' Melissa gushed, addressing Grace for the first time. 'It seems so impractical to sit at separate tables when we're all such old friends.'

'Daniel?' Grace felt duty bound to defer to him. 'I don't mind if you don't.'

With a brief nod, Daniel indicated to the waiter to leave the menus on the table.

'That's all arranged, then,' Melissa said. 'Now Daniel, tell me about your search for a new receptionist. In fact I might know the very person, now Grace has found the job too much for her. One of my customers is looking for a little job to pass the time. It would suit her down to the ground.

'I mean it can't be very difficult, can it, answering the phone and making a few appointments?' She cast a sideways glance at Grace. 'You wouldn't mind if she could only manage part time, would you? I'm sure she could manage ten 'til three. After that, of course, she would need to be around to collect the children from school.'

'So how do you know Melissa?' Jason asked Grace, squeezing her hand in sympathy. 'Take no notice,' he murmured in her ear bending his head to hers and to her surprise giving her a kiss. 'My mother always says a kiss makes everyone feel better.'

'We were at college together,' Melissa butted in, looking slightly annoyed with Jason. 'Grace dropped out before she could complete her course, but I went ahead and qualified. Grace now works in a shop,' she added, 'the local post office actually,' she trilled, 'serving sweets and stamps.'

'My mother plays bridge with the MacPherson sisters,' Jason informed Grace. 'She says they're demons at it.'

'They tried to get me to play,' Grace replied, 'but I'm not very good at cards.'

'Perhaps you'll be lucky in love, then,' Jason said.

'Do you know?' Melissa leaned across the table, her violet eyes reminding Grace of a cat's as she said, 'Grace actually thought Daniel and I were engaged?'

'Really?' Jason didn't sound in the least bit interested.

'We weren't, of course, were we?' Melissa smiled at Daniel, 'but Grace tried to split us up by kissing Daniel down by the lake on the night of the prom concert. Of course we can laugh about it now, but I was pretty annoyed at the time. I mean he was my date for the evening and there's such a thing as being loyal to your friends.'

Jason picked up one of the menus and passed it to Grace, leaving Daniel to sort out the other for Melissa.

'What do you fancy?' he asked, then dipping his head behind the menu whispered, 'apart from Melissa's head on a bit of toast?'

* * *

'Tell Charlie to get in touch with me when he's got a moment, Grace.' Jason produced a card as they finished up with coffee in the lounge. 'He can contact me on any of those numbers. I might even be interested in his business opportunity. Now I've finished my degree I'm looking round for new opportunities. I could set up a profes-sional proposal for him and make the right noises at financial people. I've got loads of connections.'

Grace slipped the card into her clutch bag. 'I'll do that. I know Charlie would love to see you again. I'm not speaking out of turn when I say he doesn't possess the sharpest of business brains. I'm sure he could do with some guidance.'

'I suppose,' Jason hesitated. 'I mean I know I'm a bit younger than you, but,' his young face coloured up, 'would you fancy going out one evening? We could visit Charlie's old stomping ground down by the marina. Perhaps go out on a boat? There might even be some of the old crowd still around.'

'That would be a lovely idea.' Grace felt touched by his suggestion. 'You've got my number, haven't you? Give me a call.'

'Better than that,' he winked, 'I'll come into the shop and buy some sweets. Tell me do you sell gobstoppers?'

He glanced at Melissa and they both broke into laughter.

'What's so funny?' Daniel demanded, moving closer to Grace, effectively relegating Melissa to the far chair.

'Jason and I were fixing up a date.'

Grace enjoyed informing Daniel. 'He and Charlie used to go surfing together.'

'I'm sorry about Melissa,' Daniel murmured. 'She collared me in the bar. I couldn't get away from her.'

'In that case,' Jason said overhearing the aside, 'come on, Melissa.' Displaying a firmness of voice that surprised even Melissa, she got to her feet as Jason added, 'It's time I drove you home. You need your beauty sleep and Daniel and Grace have hardly had a chance to talk to each other all evening.'

'I haven't monopolised things, have I?' Melissa pretended to be surprised.

'Get your coat,' Jason said firmly, 'we're leaving.'

'I hope my packet arrives at its destination tomorrow,' Melissa cast a parting shot at Grace. 'If it doesn't I'll be holding you personally responsible.'

'Good night, Melissa. I'm sure there's no need to worry,' Grace replied, 'but if you want to claim, I'll find you a form.'

'Daniel.' Melissa turned to him. 'You really must let me treat you to dinner next time. The trout cooked with almonds here is delicious. It's the chef's signature dish. Do we have a date?'

'I'm going to be rather busy in the next few weeks.'

'I'm sure you'll find a window.' She kissed him lightly on the cheek. 'I should warn you I rarely take no for an answer.'

'See you, Grace. Bye, Daniel,' Jason called over his shoulder. 'Come along.' He hustled Melissa out of the lounge.

'More coffee?' Daniel held up the pot.

'Better not. I won't sleep.' Grace stifled a yawn. 'It's been a lovely evening. Thank you, Daniel.'

'I'm sorry it didn't turn out quite how I planned. It was meant to be a thank you for rescuing Foxy.'

'Are you really going to employ Melissa's friend as your new receptionist?' Grace asked, wishing she had the courage to demand her old job back.

'I doubt it very much. I'm actually looking for someone with business qualifications,' Daniel replied.

Any last hopes Grace harboured in that direction sank. Her qualifications were of the practical variety. She had nothing on paper. If only her silly pride hadn't got the better of her, she would still be doing the job she loved and with a little give and take on both sides, maybe things might have worked out with Daniel.

'I hope you can find someone suitably qualified in Fieldling,' Grace replied. 'It's only a small village.'

'I actually have someone in mind already,' Daniel sipped his coffee.

'You do?'

'She worked with me on one of my student placements and was very helpful. I contacted her to see if she was interested and she said she was.' He smiled. 'So it looks like the problem's solved. I must say it's been quite a challenge answering the phone and trying to keep the waiting room in order. I'm not blaming you for walking out,' Daniel explained. 'It was partly my fault for being so pig-headed. I just wish you'd given me a little notice.'

'I would offer to help until my replacement arrives,' Grace said, 'but Amelia and her sister are off on holiday to Devon next week so I'll be the only cover in the shop.'

'Not to worry. I'm sure I'll manage. By the way,' Daniel looked a little embarrassed as he said, 'I heard Jason complimenting you on your dress.'

'Yes?' Grace looked at him with a puzzled frown, her heart thumping nervously. Surely he wasn't going to give her a compliment too?

'I think you turned his head,' he said with a smile. 'You know he's only twenty?'

'Actually he's twenty-one and if you're suggesting I was leading him on . . . '

'Nothing of the sort,' Daniel protested. 'Only he is younger than you.'

'He's an old friend of my brother's. He's a lovely boy and he paid me a lot more attention this evening than you did.'

'I already explained about Melissa.'

'If we're into criticism I could accuse you of much more. At least Jason wasn't clinging on to my arm.'

'He kissed you. You can't deny it. I saw him.'

'Only because Melissa was,' Grace made a gesture with her hands, 'being Melissa. Anyway if I feel like going out with Jason, then it is absolutely none of your business. Now if you're ready, I'd like to go home, please,' she added.

Daniel got slowly to his feet. 'As you wish,' he said, signalling to a waiter for his coat. 'We don't seem to have much luck at the country club, do we? You wouldn't fancy some pub grub next time?'

Grace blinked. 'I'm not sure there is going to be a next time,' she said carefully.

She felt a vicarious thrill of pleasure as she saw the surprise in his eyes.

'I'm going to have to find another job once Amelia and her sister return.'

She held her breath. Now was his chance. If Daniel didn't offer her old job back she knew things really were over between them.

'Your coat, sir.' The waiter reappeared and helped him into his jacket.

Grace picked up her clutch bag. The moment was lost. She could tell by the expression on Daniel's face that she had placed him in an embarrassing position.

'Ready?' It hurt to smile, but Grace had done it before, it was only a case of getting used to it and experience had taught her there was nothing you couldn't get used to if you put your mind to it.

Meeting Foxy Again

'Hi, sis. How are things doing? I thought I'd just give you a call to catch up.'

'Charlie,' Grace greeted her brother down the telephone as she settled back on the sofa and eased off her shoes to rub her aching feet.

It had been the usual frantic Sunday morning in the shop and Grace who had been on her own because the weekend help had telephoned in sick, was pleased to close up at two o'clock. Now she was looking forward to a lazy afternoon. A telephone chat with her brother was exactly the right therapy to start things off.

'To what do I owe the pleasure of this call?'

'Just touching base. Mum said to say hello. She and Philippe have gone shopping to stock up on supplies. They've a busy week coming up. It's the local Fête des Fleurs so they're fully booked. Honestly, I've never seen so many displays of wild orchids.'

'You'll be busy then, too?' Grace teased him. 'Making beds? Washing up?'

'I've been setting up a business plan, actually,' Charlie replied in a lofty tone, ignoring the dig.

'Oh yes?'

'I know you've heard it all before, but this time I mean it, sis.'

'Convince me.'

'Philippe's been a tremendous help introducing me to all sorts of influential people. They're making encouraging noises and have invited me to submit a detailed business plan of my venture, but before I take the thing further I need more backing. So I'm busy being nice to all the local dignitaries. I could really do with someone in England to help out, too.'

'I've got just the person.' Grace reached out for her bag.

'You have?' Charlie's voice was filled with surprise.

137

'Remember Jason Jackson?'

'JJ? Of course I do. What he's up to these days?'

'He is looking for a business opportunity.'

'No kidding? I'm your man,' Charlie jumped in enthusiastically before Grace had a chance to explain. 'If my memory serves me correctly he had a serious legacy from his grandfather and he's got a good business brain on him. Couldn't be better. Where did you meet him?'

'I bumped into him the other night and he gave me his card and said to remember him to you next time we were in touch, so I'm obeying orders.'

'You are the best sister in the world, you know that?' Charlie said after Grace had read out Jason's details for Charlie to write down.

'Naturally,' she agreed with a laugh. 'How's your lovely girlfriend, Odile?'

'She sends you her love. How are things with you? Any luck on the job front?'

'I'm full time in the shop for the next week because the sisters have gone visiting an old friend and it looks like the temporary help we hired is going to be a no show.'

'Are you sure you don't want me to have a word with Daniel about that parking fine business? He might offer you your old job back when he realises it was nothing to do with you.'

'It wouldn't do any good, Charlie, he's got someone in mind for the position so I believe, and even if he hadn't, he's looking for someone with business qualifications. I don't have any.'

'Don't put yourself down,' Charlie sounded annoyed. 'There are things that only life can teach you and you've got to admit it's thrown quite a bit of stuff at us and Mum over the past few years, and after a few hiccups we've all pulled through.'

'I'll start looking properly when Amelia and Beattie get back from Devon.'

'Well, if you need me to put in a good word for you, let me know. Listen. I'd better go. I'm on Philippe's mobile.'

'What?' Grace screeched. 'Why didn't you tell me?'

'He left it behind before he went out shopping and I can't find mine so I borrowed his.'

'Without his permission?' Grace stifled her irritation.

'I'm sure he won't mind.'

'Don't forget to ring Jason,' Grace said hastily before she cut the call. She didn't want Philippe's mobile running out of credit. For all his fine words Charlie could still take other people for granted. He didn't mean to, he just didn't think.

Grace stretched out on the sofa and cat napped as the afternoon sun played across her face. Half an hour later she awoke with a stretch, then her conscience kicked in.

She had never been one for sitting around doing nothing and it really was far too nice a day to stay indoors. Now her feet had stopped aching, her head needed clearing and a breath of fresh air and a brisk walk would do the trick she decided.

Suitably dressed for a country stroll in over-shirt and jeans, Grace ambled down the main street enjoying the pleasures and quiet of the Sunday afternoon.

All the stores were closed and it was nice to be able to walk along the pavement unimpeded by shoppers. Fieldling was a well-known centre for antiques and dealers came from far and wide to see what was on offer.

A lot of her father's artefacts had been bought up by traders with an eye for a bargain and Grace guessed they had been sold on for vast profit at one of the fairs. The thought no longer grieved her. Her life at Sycamore House was now no more than a pleasant memory and warm friendship was worth more than all the antiques in the world.

She paused outside the bakery and

looked across the road. There was no way she could leave the village without actually passing Sycamore House. It fronted onto the road, all of its acreage being at the rear.

Grace had walked past it many times since her mother had sold up, but today she couldn't help wondering if Daniel was at home or perhaps he was out somewhere with Melissa Harper. She had no idea what they had been talking about that night at the Country Club, but Melissa's intention was plain. She was making a play for Daniel and she didn't look the type of girl to do failure.

Grace knew Melissa's sister lived in a neighbouring village, easily accessible by car and Melissa drove a racy little red number. She wondered briefly if it was a parting gift from her ex-fiancé.

Whatever, it wasn't parked on the pavement outside Sycamore House so it didn't look like she was visiting. The on site property parking area, like the gardens was to the back of the property. Grace supposed on reflection Melissa could have driven through the stone archway leading round to the rear gardens.

Determinedly looking the other way and deciding she had better things to think about than Melissa and Daniel, Grace decided to stroll along the bridleway. It was easier going on the flat, rather than climbing up to the old mound, a local beauty spot and a popular meeting place in earlier times for courting couples.

With its spectacular views across the Downs, it was small wonder it was still widely visited by casual ramblers and the more hardy types who thought nothing of completing a ten-mile hike of an afternoon.

Grace ducked down the shortcut leading to the bridleway then paused as she came out into the sunlight. The dewpond was a favourite spot of hers. She and Charlie often used to play in the beech woods when they were children, then enjoy their picnic on the grass.

It was peaceful by the dewpond and Grace sat down on a stone and sipped some of her bottled water. Dewponds were a heritage of the days when Sussex shepherds tended their flocks, hardly speaking to a soul for weeks. The ponds provided fresh water for the sheep to drink from.

Refreshed, Grace stood up and decided to walk the long way round to the churchyard then double back along the bridleway. She passed several mounted riders, all of who greeted her in a friendly manner.

'Excuse me,' one rider called out. 'Is that your dog? Only he seems to be in distress.'

Grace looked to where the girl was pointing. Whimpering, Foxy limped towards her.

'It's Foxy,' she said.

'Daniel Stafford's dog?'

'Yes. Did you pass Daniel in the lane?'

'We didn't see anyone, but if you like I'll keep an eye out for him and tell him what's happened.'

Grace waved her thanks then bent down to look at Foxy's leg. 'What have you done?' she asked in a gentle voice.

Foxy licked her hand. Grace felt around his sturdy body. She couldn't see any physical injury and now he'd found a sympathetic ear, Foxy seemed to perk up. He wagged his tail and began to explore her espadrilles with his nose.

'Are you playing me up?' she demanded, 'because if you are, you can walk home on your own.'

Grace stood up and looked round. There was no sign of Daniel. In fact there was no sign of anyone. Where could he be? And if he hadn't brought Foxy out for a walk, who had?

She cupped her hands. 'Daniel?' she called out.

There was no reply. 'Daniel?' she tried again but her only response was a flapping of wings in the branches overhead.

Feeling in the pocket of her jeans

Grace found an old piece of string, which she tied around Foxy's collar.

'Come on, Foxy,' she tugged him away from the long grass. 'Best get you home then we'll decide what to do.'

Snuffling happily and no longer limping, Foxy trotted along beside Grace, occasionally straining at the leash when he smelt something of interest in the wayside.

Abandoning her plans to visit the Norman church, Grace cut across the back way, to a tiny twitten that led to the high street. She glanced at her watch. It was half past four. If Daniel had been out for the afternoon, he might be back.

Foxy gave a little bark of acknowledgement sensing he was on home territory and began tugging again at the makeshift lead.

'No you don't.' Grace tugged back. 'I'm not having you running out in front of another car and risking getting another bump on the head. We'll do this properly in a dignified manner, by using the pedestrian crossing.'

Sensing defeat, Foxy allowed himself to be led across the road. Moments later the pair of them were standing on the doorstep of Sycamore House. Grace swallowed the lump of nervousness in her throat. How would she react to seeing inside her old home again? She hadn't set foot inside the house since the bank had repossessed it, a day she didn't care to remember.

The doorbell echoed down the corridor. There was no reply. If Daniel was in the garden he might not realise Foxy was missing. She tried the bell again, but with no success.

'What we need is a telephone,' she informed Foxy. 'We'll have to go home. I left my mobile on the kitchen table. Come on, we can't wait here for ever.'

Listening in frustration to Daniel's recorded voice on the answer phone, Grace left a message informing him that she had found Foxy wandering through the woods and that he was quite safe and that he could pick his dog up any time he liked.

Moments later the telephone rang.

'Daniel?' She snatched it up.

'Hello, dear. Amelia MacPherson here.'

'Miss MacPherson.' Grace found it difficult to disguise her disappointment.

'Were you expecting someone else?'

'Not really. How are you?'

'We're having a lovely time. We went out to the local craft centre after lunch then we indulged in a cream tea. I don't think we'll be bothering with supper. The scones were absolutely delicious, better than anything I could ever bake. Beattie and I were extremely greedy. We finished the whole plateful.'

'Good for you. Now you make sure you rest up and don't worry about a thing here.'

'Is everything all right in the shop?'

'No problems,' Grace assured her. There was no need to mention the temporary's non-appearance, she decided. The sisters would only fret.

'In that case we'll see you next weekend. You've got our number for emergencies?'

After assuring them that she had replaced the receiver, then set about cooking some supper and seeing what she could find for Foxy to eat.

'I hope you're not on a diet.' She looked down at the empty bowl after Foxy had demolished the remains of a casserole Amelia had left for Grace. 'I ought to charge you board and lodging.' Foxy thumped the kitchen floor with his tail and looked up at her with adoring eyes. 'Because if your master doesn't telephone soon, it looks as though you'll be spending the night with me.'

She began to lock up for the evening then settled down on the sofa to watch one of her DVDs, a romance that always made her feel good. Soon Foxy was snoring happily by her side and Grace was trying not to let the emotion of the story get to her. She sighed happily at the end of the film as the credits rolled.

'Did you enjoy that, Foxy?'

She received a snuffled reply from the depths of the cushions.

'Much as I hate to disturb your

lordship, you can't go to sleep yet. We are going to have to go out briefly for your evening walk. Come on. We'll see if anyone's in at Sycamore House.'

The house was in darkness. Grace frowned. She was puzzled. Where was Daniel?

'Who was supposed to be looking after you, Foxy?' she asked. 'And why were you running around in the woods on your own?'

With one last look through one of Sycamore House's windows, Grace retraced her steps up the high street.

'You'd better sleep in the kitchen, Foxy. I'm sure there's an old basket somewhere so you'll be nice and warm. Don't forget to bark if we get intruders, will you? No licking them and making them feel welcome. You hear?'

Grace did a last minute check for telephone messages and seeing that there weren't any, she closed the door on Foxy and went upstairs to bed.

'You're An Incomer'

Rain trickled down the shop front window. Low grey clouds darkened the sky. It was heavy with the promise of more rain. Shoppers hurried past, unable to control their umbrellas.

Several had blown inside out. Grace sighed. She hated days like this. After yesterday's sunshine it was such a contrast. Water escaped through a gap in the overhead guttering creating a relentless stream that was steadily getting on her nerves.

Grace had left Foxy snuggled up in the makeshift basket she had set up in the kitchen and right now she felt like joining him. After the initial early-morning rush for newspapers and sandwiches there had been a dearth of customers and Grace was growing fidgety. She hated having nothing to do.

Where was Daniel? She had tried his

number again that morning but without success.

Unable to sit still any longer she began to tidy up the magazines and periodicals. The ping of the doorbell provided a welcome distraction.

'Don't move,' a voice behind her said.

'What?' Grace's knee cracked as she straightened up. 'Sorry, I get cramp if I don't ease it out.' She hobbled around on one leg grabbing out at a shelf. A packet of loose sugar fell to the floor and split open spilling its contents. Her feet made crunching noises as she tried to steady herself. She stiffened up again as something was nudged into her back.

'I said don't move.'

She spun round and bumped into a slender youth in a hooded jacket. He looked more nervous than confrontational.

'I'll do exactly as I like,' she retaliated. 'It's my shop and I'm in charge so what I say goes.'

The statement wasn't strictly true. It

was Amelia and Beattie's shop, but this wasn't the time for explanations. Grace took in her visitor's dishevelled appearance. The lad was wet through. Water dripped off his wax jacket and was forming a puddle of water on the floor. He looked as miserable as the weather.

'What do you want?' she asked with a trace of sympathy.

Before she could reply another male voice jerked him round. 'I'd like to know the answer to that question as well.'

'Nothing.' The youth began to panic as he realised it was now two against one. 'I don't want nothing.'

'Except perhaps a lesson in grammar?' Daniel enquired.

'What?' The jacket the youth was wearing fell open and Grace saw to her relief that he had only nudged her with his fisted hand, hardly a weapon of mass destruction.

'No need to make a scene,' Grace said, anxious to downplay the incident, 'and no harm done.'

Both males ignored her.

'I suggest you apologise to Miss Maxwell then take yourself off, unless of course she wants to take the matter further.'

'I can handle this, thank you, Daniel,' Grace insisted, pleased he had come to her defence, but annoyed that he seemed to be taking charge of things.

'No, you can't,' Daniel said with a mutinous thrust to his jaw.

'Yes, I can, and there's no need to be quite so heavy handed with the boy. Can't you see he's not much more than a child? What did you come here for?' Grace demanded of the boy. 'You still haven't answered my question.'

He hung his head.

'Answer Miss Maxwell,' Daniel ordered him.

Grace glared at him. 'Look,' she touched the wet sleeve of the boy's jacket, 'if it's money you're after, then this isn't the way to get it. You've got to earn it.' The hood of his jacket slipped off his head and Grace could see he suffered from teenage acne. Her anger softened.

'Sorry, miss,' he stumbled over the apology. He looked ready to cry. 'It was a dare. They're all laughing at me,' he jerked his head towards where there should have been a queue for the school bus. It had disappeared as if by magic.

'Why are they laughing at you?' Grace asked.

'I haven't got any money for computer games and things. My dad's stopped my school allowance 'cos my exam results were bad.'

Grace's heart went out to him.

'And that's why they were teasing you?'

He nodded wordlessly. Grace thought she caught the suggestion of a tear on his eyelashes.

'Would you like some help?' she asked. 'If you're short of money.'

'What?'

'I could offer you a paper round?' Grace suggested. 'You'd have to be here on time every morning, but at the end of the week you'd have some money to spend and a sense of achievement. What do you say? You would be earning your own money. You'd be doing me a favour, too. One of my regulars has gone sick.'

'You're offering me a job?'

'I am.'

'I've never had a job before,' the boy mumbled to the floor, still blushing with a sense of guilt. 'My teacher says I'm useless.'

Grace's blood boiled. Goodness knows what harm the boy's teacher had done by telling him that.

'Then I'm giving you a chance to prove him wrong. Now do you accept my offer?'

'For real?' The young lad looked at her with hope. 'You're not having me on?'

'Of course not. What's your name?'

'Andy, Andy Malcolm.'

'You're the doctor's son, aren't you?' Grace asked after a short pause.

'You won't tell my dad, will you?' he

asked the look of panic returning.

'I won't and I'm sure we can swear Mr Stafford to secrecy, too?' Grace looked across to where Daniel was standing, his arms folded, as he took in the scene.

'You don't owe his father any favours.' He didn't look prepared to be quite so lenient.

'But you won't tell on Andy, will you?'

Daniel shook his head, his hazel eyes filled with incomprehension. Grace sensed she had won her case.

'I don't tell tales, for all my other faults,' Daniel replied. 'Andy's secret is safe with me.'

'Thank you,' she smiled back at him.

'So, Andy, are you going to accept Miss Maxwell's generous offer?' Daniel asked him.

'Don't know.' Andy didn't look too sure.

'Problem?' he quizzed the lad.

'It would mean getting up early.'

'You can manage that, can't you?' Grace asked.

'I don't mind, but my dad might

wonder what I'm up to. He's always having to drag me out of bed.'

'Then tell him,' Daniel ordered crisply.

'He knows Miss MacPherson and her sister, Mrs Beattie, doesn't he?' Grace asked.

Andy nodded.

'Then say they offered you the job.'

'But you're not Miss MacPherson.'

'I'm her representative and best not mention my name to your father,' Grace put in swiftly. 'I don't actually own the shop, despite what I said earlier, but in Miss MacPherson's absence I've got full authority to employ you.'

'All right,' Andy agreed slowly, before he broke into a happy smile. 'This has to be the best day of my life. Someone believes in me.'

Grace smiled back at him. 'I was in your position once,' she admitted.

'No kidding? Cool.'

'Although I didn't go as far as holding up a shopkeeper. All I needed was someone to believe in me too. I was given a chance so now I'm repaying the debt.'

Daniel made a faint movement, but Grace did not look at him. Right now Andy needed her whole attention.

'Thanks, Miss Maxwell. You are an ace lady.' Andy was now beaming at her. 'Like I said, I'm sorry if I spooked you. See you tomorrow.'

'Here.' She handed him some biscuits. 'Share them with your friends. They'll be doubly impressed when you tell them you talked your way into a job.'

'I did, didn't I?' Andy took the biscuits then with hardly a look at Daniel he careered out of the shop.

Outside the sun began to break through the rain clouds and Grace watched him race off towards the bus stop to where the group of youngsters had miraculously reappeared. Moments later the school bus drew up. The doors opened and a new full of confidence Andy leapt on board.

159

'That was quite some performance,' Daniel congratulated her. 'You did a good thing there, too.'

'Until you came in I was actually quaking,' Grace confessed, 'I had to pretend to have cramp, that's why there's sugar all over the floor.'

'I can't see the connection.' Daniel looked puzzled. 'But there's no need to explain. As long as you're not harmed?'

'I'm fine — careful where you step, by the way. I'll clean it up in a minute.'

'You really don't owe Andy Malcolm anything,' Daniel stepped over the mess on the floor, 'especially after the way his father treated you.'

'As I said, I'm repaying my debt to Miss MacPherson. She gave me my first chance when no-one else had much good to say about my family,' Grace replied, anxious to move the subject away from the doctor.

'Well, I hope Andy turns up tomorrow morning.'

'He will.' Grace was certain on that one. 'I've given him some street cred.

You know, respect?'

'You're making me feel very old, with all this modern speak.' Daniel looked hard into her face. 'You're sure you're all right?' he asked in concern. 'Andy didn't scare you?'

'I'm glad you came in when you did,' Grace admitted, 'but no, he didn't scare me.'

'Good, because I probably would have spilt more than sugar on the floor if he had.'

'Then you would have had to clear it up and explain to Miss MacPherson exactly what you were doing trashing her stock.'

'I would have been defending your honour,' Daniel said in a slow voice full of meaning.

Grace blinked up at him and hoped he wasn't going to try to kiss her by way of sympathy or anything like that. She wasn't sure her immune system was up to it. It was only Monday morning, but she'd had enough real life experiences to last her the week.

'Have you come to collect Foxy?' she asked.

'Yes. I've been away for the weekend visiting my sister in London. I only got back this morning. Melissa said she'd look after Foxy for me. Where did you find him?'

'Running around the woods. Some horse riders saw him. We thought he'd injured his paw, but it was nothing. Luckily Foxy recognised me, so I said I'd look after him. We walked back to your house. I knocked on your front door but there was no reply.'

'I would have been back last night, but I needed to see someone this morning.'

'I brought Foxy back here and gave him a bed for the night.'

'Then I owe you another one,' Daniel said, 'for yet again rescuing Foxy. At least this time you didn't bump your head or get a black eye.'

'Have you heard from Melissa?' Grace asked.

'There was a message asking me to

ring her, but I came straight over here after I heard your messages. I'll call her later.' Daniel was no longer smiling. 'I dread to think what could have happened to him.'

Grace turned the sign on the door round to closed. 'He's in the kitchen. Come on through.'

Foxy greeted his master with rapturous delight and for a few moments the scene in the kitchen was chaotic.

'Yes, yes,' Daniel fondled the silky ears. 'I'm pleased to see you, too. Now settle down. I need to talk to Grace.'

Foxy padded back to his basket and curled up on one of the cushions.

'The thing is . . . ' Daniel cleared his throat as he sat down at the pine table. 'The reason I was delayed in London an extra night was that acquaintance I mentioned, the one who was interested in the receptionist's job?'

'What about her?'

'I had an appointment with her this morning.'

Grace paused from pouring hot water

on to the coffee granules.

'Did you offer her the job?'

'She is highly qualified and eminently suitable.'

'I sense a 'but',' Grace said.

'There's a big difference between being a London-based vet's assistant and a country one.'

'Have you only just realised that?'

'I'm not sure her credentials are quite right for Fieldling.'

'I see.'

'People have been deserting the practice wholesale since you left.'

'I'm sorry to hear that.'

'It's getting to the situation where I've got no advance appointments.'

'Are you going to leave, too?' Grace felt a lump of despair in the pit of her stomach. This was all her fault.

'That could be up to you.'

'Come again?'

'I think we got off on the wrong foot, my fault as much as yours. I mean if you hadn't parked in Dr Malcolm's space and got yourself on the front pages of the local press and I hadn't been so intent on having either an automated system or a receptionist with qualifications we might not be in the position we are.'

Grace nudged a mug of tea towards Daniel.

'Sugar's on the shop floor, I suppose?' he asked with the suggestion of a smile.

''Fraid so.'

'Just as well I don't take it then, isn't it?'

They smiled at each other.

'So where do we stand?' Grace asked eventually.

'Do you want your old job back?' Daniel asked. 'I'll concede defeat on the notice board. It stays. I will admit it does have a certain usefulness. For my part I would like to introduce one or two new practices, if you think they would fit in of course,' Daniel added, a muscle tweaking at the corner of his mouth. 'I've never known such a place as Fieldling for clinging to tradition. The slightest change and the whole place goes into trauma.'

'We move with the times.' Grace leapt to the defence of her village.

'I'm sure you do,' Daniel agreed hastily, 'but I'm finding it difficult to get anyone to listen to my suggestions.'

'That's because you're an incomer.'

'You mean I have to live here thirty years before anyone takes me seriously?'

'Something like that.'

'In that case, I need help.'

Grace's heart was thumping so fast it hurt her breastbone.

'I've promised Miss MacPherson I'll run the shop until the end of the week, while she's away.'

'I've temporarily closed the surgery,' Daniel said. 'I need to sort things out. You could start next Monday, couldn't you? Unless you'd like some time off?'

'I've just had a holiday in France.'

'In that case?'

A furious tapping on the back window interrupted them.

'Not another teenager with attitude.' Daniel raised his eyes.

'Probably an anxious customer wanting to know why I've closed up.'

'In that case I'll leave through the front of the shop. If there's a queue outside I can explain it was my fault. Come on, Foxy, say thank you to Grace, then we'll be on our way.'

To Grace's surprise, Melissa was hovering on the step. She looked stunning in a bright yellow raincoat, her hair not in the least bit flattened by the wet weather.

'There you are.' She fell into Daniel's arms. 'I've been so worried about Foxy. Why didn't you answer my messages? I was up half the night looking for him. I'm so glad he's safe. Darling,' she bent down to pat the dog.

Foxy growled and backed away.

'Silly dog. It's me,' Melissa said with a tinkling laugh. She stood up. 'Grace, you really should have rung me to let me know you'd kidnapped him.'

'I didn't know you were supposed to be looking after him,' Grace replied. 'After I found him I called out but no-one was around. I couldn't leave him.'

'Found him? Where?' Melissa's almond eyes narrowed.

'No need to go into all that now,' Daniel replied. 'No harm done. Melissa, as you can see, Foxy is fine. We'd better leave Grace in peace. She's had a busy morning.'

'Anything you say,' Melissa agreed with alacrity.

'Did your parcel arrive safely?' Grace asked her, having already checked.

'What? Oh yes, thank you.' She dismissed the question as if it was of no importance.

'You'll ring me your decision tonight?' Daniel asked.

'What decision is this?' Melissa demanded.

'Daniel's offered me my old job back and subject to benefits,' Grace informed her, 'I may accept.'

'Your job back?' Melissa looked scandalised. 'Surely not.'

'Benefits?' Daniel demanded. 'What do you mean?'

'I mean a raise in salary,' Grace smiled sweetly, 'in keeping with the new image you want to portray? You surely weren't thinking of offering less than the going rate?' Grace wanted to laugh at the expression on both their faces.

'Er, yes, right, fine, whatever you say,' Daniel agreed hastily. 'Do we have a deal?'

Melissa looked as though she were about to burst with indignation.

'I'll call you tonight,' Grace replied and turned the sign around to read 'Open'. And now if you'll excuse me, I must get back to selling my stamps and sweets.'

An Ill-Timed Encounter

The smell of new paint made Grace's nostrils twitch. She opened a window to let in some fresh air before she had a sneezing fit, then she looked around in approval. The pastel shades were very restful and opened out the office space, but she wasn't sure exactly how practical a colour pale lemon was. In her experience the walls would soon show up every mark and scuff. Sick pets were no respecters of interior design.

Daniel had used the chance to have the surgery repainted in her absence and the decorators had moved in while the practice was temporarily closed. His workstation now looked cleaner and fresher with its new layout and up-to-date information system. Decorating was a job Mr Vincent always meant to get round to but had never found the time.

Grace was pleased to see her old desk had been left in situ. She liked its lived-in appearance, the comfortable way it took up an entire corner of the reception area and the big wooden drawers she used to hide away all the bits and pieces she had accumulated over the years. The notice board was exactly where she had left it. It had been wiped clean and now stood in its usual corner awaiting new messages.

Grace sat down on her office chair and twirled it round. Daniel had given her a day to settle in before the surgery opened in earnest. He was out on a call and told her he didn't expect to be back so if she wanted to arrange anything in his absence, as long as it wasn't too drastic, then to go ahead.

A broad smile stretched across her face. She hadn't realised quite how much she'd missed the work. The paintwork hadn't entirely eradicated the old animal smells of rabbit fur and damp dog, and Grace was pleased about that. She didn't want things too clinical, but she hadn't plucked up the courage to tell Daniel. Now it looked as though it wasn't going to be necessary.

The surgery had originally been a small, purpose-built medical centre situated on a rural industrial estate on the outskirts of Fieldling. A convenient bus route served it, stopping right outside their door. The services were regular and departed on the hour and half hour from the stop outside the post house.

Mr Vincent had taken over the unit and revamped the premises. They consisted of two offices, hers and Daniel's, a small operating theatre which doubled as a workshop, a kitchen, various store and cloakrooms and a tiny square of garden around the back.

Unless Grace overslept, it was almost impossible for her to be late for work. Most days she drove, as she liked the independence of her own transport and she occasionally ran errands for the surgery. Mr Vincent always bicycled into work so her car had been more than useful on many an occasion.

The telephone rang causing several lights to flash on the smart new intercom.

'Fieldling vet surgery,' Grace flicked a switch.

'Hello. How are you settling in?'

'Checking up on me?' she asked with a laugh, recognising Daniel's voice.

'Not at all.'

'Everything's fine. I approve.'

'That's a relief.'

'So as you can hear, I've turned up for work and I'm on time.' Grace cast a glance at the new wall clock. If anything she was a few minutes early.

'After you talked me into giving you a hefty pay rise I thought you might decide to push for more benefits to seal the deal.'

'I wouldn't do that,' Grace was quick to insist. 'I've signed my new contract and it's in my bag to give to you.'

She had suffered a tweak of conscience over the success of her negotiating skills, but then decided if Daniel was prepared to pay the same salary to someone new, then she was definitely worth the increased offer. There was no denying the extra money would come in useful.

'Good, well, I'll be out all day visiting. If anyone telephones we're open for business again as from tomorrow so you can start making appointments. You'd better get in a supply of refreshments.'

'Does the budget run to biscuits for the patients?' Grace couldn't resist asking. She had no doubt there would be something of a party atmosphere during her first week in office.

'It does,' Daniel replied, 'and I like chocolate creams.'

Glad he had given in to all her demands, Grace drove to the nearest town to visit the bank in order to sign the necessary papers for the new business account he had set up, then on to the supermarket to get the shopping for the surgery.

As she drove along she mulled over

the events of the past week. Much to her surprise, young Andy Malcolm had been on the doorstep of the post office bright and early the morning following their encounter.

His father it seemed had raised no objection to his son doing a paper round and Andy had proved to be a reliable, efficient and thoughtful young man. It was only by accident Grace discovered he had volunteered to do some light shopping for Mrs Watts and had also put his name down on the rota for mowing the vicarage lawn.

Amelia MacPherson had also been delighted too to discover Andy was prepared to open the shop for her if she was late down and had actually entrusted him with a key.

'He's a treasure, Grace. I'm so glad you found him. A strong young man about the place is a useful asset, I must say.'

Beattie and Amelia had at first been cautious over Grace's news that she was returning to the surgery, but they had both come round to the idea when

Grace suggested they invite Daniel round for Sunday tea to discuss plans for the new practice.

She'd watch him really listening to the sisters' suggestions as to how best run the revamped surgery. Grace knew as lifelong village residents their input was important and she had been pleased Daniel had not patronised them.

He had taken several of their suggestions on board and Grace fully expected their patient list to return to its previous healthy level.

Grace wandered down the super-market aisle her head full of various innovations she had in mind to imple-ment. She didn't notice a trolley bumping hers until their wheels ground against each other.

'Hi, there.' The owner of the second trolley greeted her. 'Feeling hungry?' He nodded down at her plentiful supply of biscuits.

'Jason,' she greeted him. 'Sorry, I was miles away.'

He kissed her on the cheek. 'I can see

that. So the rumour is true? You are back at the surgery?'

'Yes.'

'Melissa's not best pleased about that. I bumped into her the other day. She was telling me some story about you kidnapping Daniel's dog and pretending she'd lost it in order to get back into his good books. It all sounded a bit far fetched to me, so I didn't pay that much attention.'

'Never mind Melissa.' Grace leaned towards Jason. 'Have you been in touch with Charlie?'

'I was going to ring you about that. I have and I'm going out there to meet Philippe and to discuss our business venture.'

'That's wonderful news.'

'Charlie's sourced some premises near Menton. Of course we are only in the very early discussion stages. Some parts of the Mediterranean aren't that ideal for windsurfing and paragliding because the water's too calm, but we thought we could set up a sort of school for novices and run courses, with a bit of practical thrown in to build up people's confidence.'

'That's an excellent idea.'

'So you're looking at an entrepreneur.' Jason stretched out his arms proudly to emphasise his status. 'Whoops, sorry, madam,' he laughed as he nearly hit another shopper in the face. 'I'm showing off,' he informed her.

Merely raising her eyebrows at Grace, the woman wandered off down the aisle.

'Behave,' Grace chided him. 'I don't want to get evicted from the supermarket on my first day back at the surgery.'

'Fancy celebrating tonight?' Jason asked. 'My new venture with your brother, Charlie, and your reinstatement as official surgery receptionist? We could go down to the marina?'

'That would be lovely.'

'Pick you up at eight. Better get on. For goodness sake,' he frowned, 'why do the wheels on these things never seem to go in the same direction at the same time?' He collided with yet another shopper as he tried to sort out his trolley.

'Next week my mother can do the family shopping herself.' He ground his teeth as he met with further resistance. 'I shall be sunning myself in the south of France. Bye, darling.' He blew Grace a kiss. 'Don't forget our date.'

She smiled at his retreating back as he scooted off down the aisle. Turning back to her own trolley she bumped into yet another shopper.

'Up to your old tricks, I see?'

Dressed in a crisp lime blouse and tailored matching slacks, Melissa looked ready for the catwalk rather than a supermarket sweep.

'I suppose if things don't work out with Daniel, you've got Jason to fall back on.'

'My relationship with both Daniel and Jason is purely professional.'

'Clearly we have different professional standards. I must say yours seem to work. Perhaps I should forsake my principles, too.'

'Look, Melissa, do we have to keep up this silly feud? What happened between you and Daniel was over a long time ago and I've no wish to interfere with any new relationship between you.'

Melissa's almond eyes narrowed. 'I heard you making a date with Jason,' she said.

Grace blinked. Perhaps it would be a good idea to pretend there was something between her and Jason. That way she would not be compromising Daniel or Melissa.

'Well, yes.' She pretended to be flustered. 'We are going out tonight.'

Grace hoped Melissa had not heard their exchange about the proposed business set up between Charlie and Jason.

'And there really is nothing of a personal nature between you and Daniel?'

'He's my employer, that's all.'

The hard expression on Melissa's face softened fractionally. 'I'm sorry about Foxy,' she said. 'We went for a walk and somehow or other we got separated. My sister and I drove around for ages looking for him.'

Her account of what happened did not explain why Melissa had tried to put the blame on Grace, but she was pleased they were at least trying to be polite to each other so she accepted the apology for the olive branch it was.

'Good. Well, I'd better get on.' Grace made the first move.

'Is today your first day at the surgery?' Melissa asked.

'Yes.' She indicated the contents of her trolley. 'That's why I'm stockpiling tea and coffee. Pop in if you feel like it. The door will always be open.'

'Thanks. I might just do that.'

Melissa's mobile rang creating a welcome interruption. She waved a manicured hand at Grace as she took the call and Grace seized her chance to make her escape.

She piled her shopping into the boot of her car and took a deep breath. It was almost lunchtime. Miss MacPherson had suggested they share a bowl of soup. With a brief stop to deliver her shopping to the surgery, Grace drove back to the post house and parked in the road outside.

'Miss MacPherson, Amelia?' she called out.

Another change in their relationship had taken place over the weekend when Andy popped in to see them and to introduce himself properly to the sisters. To Grace's amazement Miss MacPherson had seemed rather thrilled when the young boy had called her by her first name and after he had gone, she insisted Grace do the same.

'One must move with the times,' Amelia insisted, 'so from now on it's Beattie and Amelia.'

'Good idea.' Beattie looked up from writing the date on the new-laid eggs. 'Mrs Bishop always makes me think of my late mother-in-law and much as I loved her she was rather a scary lady.'

Grace found Amelia sitting at the

kitchen table looking rather pale. The heated up soup had boiled dry in the saucepan.

'Amelia?' Grace rushed to her side. 'Are you unwell?'

'Hello, dear.' She smiled. 'Is it lunch time already? I felt a little breathless and decided to sit down. I had no idea it was so late. Beattie's doing a stint in the mobile library and said she wouldn't be joining us for lunch. What's that smell? Good heavens, I've let the soup burn dry.'

'Would you like me to call the doctor?'

'Whatever for?' Amelia brushed aside the suggestion. 'I didn't sleep very well last night, that's all. I expect I'm still recovering from the long journey back from Devon. Now if you set the table, I'll reheat some more soup.'

Grace had been reluctant to leave Amelia after lunch, but Amelia insisted that after a brief lie down she was sure she would be fine. The soup had returned the colour to her cheeks and she seemed more her old self as she tackled the washing up.

'You'd better get back to the surgery,' she insisted. 'We don't want to give Daniel Stafford further cause to dismiss you for a second time.'

'You've got the number, haven't you?' Grace asked.

'Of course, dear, it's on the wall by the telephone, but please don't fuss so. Andy will be popping in after school so if I need any help he'll be on hand.'

There were several messages waiting for Grace at the surgery. Soon the appointments schedule was full and she spent the afternoon organising the surgery for the following day.

'So glad you're back, dear,' one of their regulars trilled, when Grace returned her call. 'I didn't like going on the bus all the way into town. Now what time did you say my appointment was?' Grace waited while the caller found her glasses then did a search for pencil and paper before finally arranging the details.

There were one or two more telephone calls after five o'clock, but eventually Grace was forced to switch on the answering machine to record any further messages. The door behind her opened as she finished entering the last appointment.

'Still here?' Daniel strode into the surgery.

'We've been busy,' Grace replied, logging off. 'I didn't think you were coming in.'

'I'm not checking up on you,' he smiled, 'but I need to collect some paperwork from my desk. I've been drumming up business too and I've run out of leaflets,' he informed her. 'I went round all the customers who deserted us and apart from one or two rather abrasive encounters I think we've got most of them back.' A smile curved his lips as he informed her. 'I think it was the lure of your notice board and a plentiful supply of biscuits.'

'Then you'd better stand by for a busy day tomorrow.'

Grace picked up her bag and stretched.

'Do you fancy christening the surgery?'

She stopped mid-stretch. 'Sorry?'

'A drink, later on tonight?'

Grace was annoyed to realise a flush was working its way up her neck. She thought it was something she'd grown out of.

'Actually I've got a date for tonight,' she admitted.

'Hi, Grace.' Melissa appeared in the doorway, 'you said to drop by any time, so here I am. Daniel,' she air-kissed him, 'have you had a busy day? Fancy some wild social life tonight? I would ask Grace to join us, but she's going out with her toy boy.'

'Jason, you're going out with Jason Jackson?' Daniel asked.

'Didn't you know?' Her cheekbones stretched as Melissa smiled, the expression on her face reminding Grace of a Siamese cat. 'Yes, she and the divine Jason are an item. A very modern arrangement, wouldn't you say?'

'Is this true?' Daniel queried.

'Of course it's true,' Melissa pouted. 'Don't you believe me? I bumped into Grace in the supermarket and caught them kissing.'

By now Grace was feeling so warm, she was surprised her face hadn't caught fire.

'I am going out with Jason tonight,' she admitted.

'There you are then,' Melissa patted Daniel's arm. 'We'll leave the lovebirds to do their own thing, shall we? Once they've got to know each other better, maybe we can go out in a foursome again? I did so enjoy our last double date. You'd better get a move on, Grace,' Melissa urged her. 'It's gone six already.'

'I'll see you in the morning.' Grace tried to smile brightly, but her face hurt as she saw the expression in Daniel's eyes. It was an expression she didn't know how to interpret, but one she sensed that would not best please Melissa.

An Evening Out

Grace watched Daniel concentrating on the small furry body in front of him on the operating table. The kitten was very young and her distraught owner had brought her pet in very late in the afternoon.

'I think she's trodden on something nasty.' The woman's eyes were wide with fear. 'Glass, perhaps?' The wailing from inside the cat basket was heart-rending. 'Is Mr Stafford here?'

'Sit down.' Grace did her best to soothe the woman. 'I'll see if I can find him.'

'I was so worried he'd gone home and that I'd missed him. I know I'm late. Please can you help? Marmalade is my daughter's pet and she absolutely dotes on the animal. Sally is out at swimming club and I was supposed to be looking after her, but the baby began to cry and I dropped a bottle of milk, then my husband telephoned from work. The next thing I knew there was blood on the floor and the kitten was yowling in pain. I had to leave the baby with a neighbour. I don't know if I'm coming or going. Please can you help?'

'Don't worry,' Grace assured her. 'Mr Stafford will see to Marmalade for you.'

'It's nasty,' Daniel said as he extracted a sharp slither of glass from the soft pad underneath the cat's paw. 'I'm glad it wasn't left any longer. It could have done more serious damage if it had turned septic. The poor little mite must have been in agony.'

Grace watched him perform the delicate operation, his fingers deft and competent. She was pleased when he had asked her to assist and now enjoyed a sense of achievement as Daniel finished off.

He looked up at Grace a few moments later. 'All done.'

Grace had been unaware she was holding her breath and she let it out with a long sigh.

'You are allowed to breathe during an operation,' Daniel informed her solemnly.

'It gets to me every time,' Grace admitted with an embarrassed smile, 'Especially when they're as small as this little kitten.' She blinked hard and wished Daniel wasn't looking at her quite so intently. She would have liked to apply a tissue to her eyes.

'Why don't you go and reassure Marmalade's owner that the patient is fine, while I finish up here?' he suggested gently.

'Can she take her home?' Grace asked.

'I don't see why not as long as they keep a careful eye on her.'

'Another satisfied customer,' Grace said as she closed and locked the surgery door behind her when the woman left.

Daniel undid his apron and threw it in the laundry basket. 'It's been a busy week.'

'I've never known one like it. I'm glad it's Friday. We've completely run out of coffee and tea. I offered the last of our supplies to that lady. I'll have to go shopping over the weekend, if that's all right?'

'The weekend is supposed to be your spare time.'

'I've got to go into town anyway,' Grace assured him.

'Take the money out of petty cash then. Don't leave yourself short.'

'Are you and Melissa doing anything at the weekend?' Grace asked as she tidied up her desk.

Daniel paused. 'The position between Melissa and myself is the same as it was five years ago.'

'I, er, wasn't prying,' Grace replied, feeling unaccountably hot. Had he really thought that?

Thrown together with Daniel on a daily basis and often in intense, highly charged, one-to-one situations, her respect for him had deepened. Their business methods were diverse, but they had managed to agree on compromise, and over the past month, the mixture had worked well. The patients liked the smart new surgery and the professional image it created, but they also appreciated some of the old practices Grace had insisted they retain.

'I'm not suggesting you were prying. In fact,' Daniel went on, 'if you're free tonight I was going to suggest we celebrate the success of our new partnership.'

'Sorry?'

'That is if you're not going out with Jason Jackson?'

'The relationship between Jason and myself is that of friends, nothing more,' Grace informed him aware she was sounding equally as terse.

She was wondering how she was going to explain diplomatically that over the past five years her life had lurched from one crisis to another and now it seemed to be setting a stable course she had no wish to create ripples by getting emotionally entangled — with anyone.

'In that case as we are both free agents we could go to the new bistro?' Daniel glanced at his watch. 'I don't know about you but I'm hungry and you only had half a banana for lunch.'

Grace flushed. She didn't think Daniel had noticed she had abandoned her break due to the constant ringing of the telephone.

'I need to freshen up first.' Grace suspected her face was shiny from the heat of the overhead lights in the surgery and she was sure her mascara had run when she'd tried to surreptitiously wipe away a tear as Daniel finished the operation.

Donning a fresh blouse that she kept hanging in the cupboard, Grace repaired her make-up in the mirror and did the best she could with her hair. It was flyaway at the best of times and tonight it seemed intent on misbehaving more than usual.

'Ready?' Daniel greeted her as she emerged a few moments later.

He had changed into a casual polo shirt and chinos that he kept at the practice.

'I think so.' Grace cast one last look around the office.

'Quick then,' Daniel urged her out of the door. 'In case the telephone starts ringing again.'

Several local residents greeted them as they strolled along the high street and Grace feared the gossip that would result from the sight of them together in a relaxed and social surrounding. The rumour-mongers would probably have them engaged by tomorrow morning.

'You're very quiet.' Daniel slowed his pace to hers.

'I was thinking,' Grace smiled back at him.

'About what?'

'How things have changed at the surgery.'

It wasn't exactly a fib, she had been thinking that earlier on, but there was no way she was going to inform Daniel what she had really been thinking.

'For the better, I hope.'

'I think so.'

His fingers grazed hers and it seemed natural to continue the rest of their walk holding hands. The bistro was buzzing by the time they reached it.

'Looks like we got the last table,' Daniel said as they squeezed into a corner booth. 'This place is popular.'

Grace had already caught several inquisitive glances in their direction and a bit of nudging of elbows as they'd walked in.

'By the way, you're not still doing a double shift at the post office, are you?' Daniel said after they'd ordered. 'Your receptionist job is demanding enough.'

Grace shook her head. 'Andy's been helping out quite a bit and Amelia has employed someone new for the week-end after the previous girl let her down.'

'You were doing too much before,' Daniel said, his hazel eyes full of concern.

'I had to,' Grace admitted.

Daniel put out a hand and touched hers a gesture not lost on the occupants of the neighbouring table.

'You don't have to keep trying to make up for your family's past sins, you know.'

'I'm not.' Grace snatched her hand away and picking up a breadstick snapped it in half. She munched determinedly, daring Daniel to contradict her.

'Be that as it may,' he smiled patiently, 'I'm glad you decided to come back to work with me. I couldn't have managed the surgery on my own. The locals relate to you. I've seen them confiding in you, things they would never say to me. It's a great sign of their trust in you.'

Grace was glad the lighting in the bistro was kept low. Her complexion didn't know how to deal with the emotion churning inside her stomach and she suspected that yet again she was blushing furiously.

Their pasta arrived, creating a welcome diversion and for a few moments they ate without talking.

'How are you getting on at Sycamore House?' Grace asked eventually to break the silence between them.

'I haven't done very much to it actually,' Daniel admitted. 'The last people turned it round for a quick profit, which was just as well as I'm hardly ever there. Do you mind?'

'Mind what?'

'Me living in your old family home?'

'No.' Grace shook her head. 'Once the family broke up, we all went our separate ways. My mother has built a new life in France and Charlie's trying to set up a business with Jason Jackson actually.'

'Good for them,' Daniel said, 'you can stop feeling responsible for your younger brother now.'

Grace remembered the parking fine incident and flushed. She would have liked to explain exactly what happened, but that would mean betraying Charlie and that was something she would never do.

The waiter removed their empty plates.

'Have you room for dessert?'

'I don't think I could manage an entire portion of apple pie, although it does look nice.'

'In that case we'll share,' Daniel said,

signalling to the waiter, 'and two spoons,' he added after he'd ordered extra custard for them. 'I don't like dry apple pie,' he explained.

'Then be prepared for a jugful of custard,' Grace said, then burst out laughing, as that was exactly what was delivered to the table.

'The chef says to help yourself.' The young waiter winked at Grace. 'Custard, the food of love.'

'He made that up,' Grace insisted. 'Shall I be mother?' She poured custard over the rich crust pastry. 'Dig in,' she urged Daniel as she picked up one of the spoons.

'Want the last bit?' Daniel invited, pointing to it with his spoon.

'I couldn't. I think we were given a double portion,' Grace sighed. 'That was absolutely delicious. I may never move again.'

'I'm glad we ordered a taxi and won't have to walk or drive home. We can finish our bottle of wine with a clear conscience.'

'So if you're not seeing Melissa at the weekend what will you be doing?' Grace felt emboldened to ask.

'Paperwork, a bit of gardening. Take Foxy for a walk. My sister may bring her husband and children down from London for some country air. Exciting things like that. You?'

'The same. Shopping in town, then I've got to catch up on chores. Make some telephone calls and help in the shop on Sunday.'

'You said you didn't do that any more.' Daniel frowned.

'I sit and read all the newspapers for an hour before the relief takes over, that's all.'

'Well don't overdo things.'

'I like to help out, but I won't, I promise. How is Foxy? Has he recovered from his adventure?'

'He's actually been looking tired lately. He's taken to limping a bit, as well.'

'He was doing that the day I found him in the woods. At first I thought he had been injured, but he seemed to recover so I thought no more about it. Sorry, I should have mentioned it.'

'No matter. It's probably one of those things that will pass.'

'You're the vet.' Grace stifled a yawn. 'Sorry,' she apologised. 'Food and wine always does that to me.'

'It's been a long day, it's time you went home to bed.' Daniel picked up his glass. 'I forgot the toast. To us,' he said solemnly.

Grace chinked her glass against his. 'Can we drink to ourselves?' she asked. 'Isn't that unlucky?'

'In that case, to you,' Daniel said in a soft voice.

After a fraction of a pause, Grace echoed, 'To you.'

'There, that wasn't too difficult, was it?' Daniel smiled.

Grace looked into his eyes. Daniel would never know exactly how difficult it had been.

Jason Stakes His Claim

'I'm so sorry to bother you,' Daniel sounded extremely apologetic over the telephone, 'only it's my sister.'

Grace stretched and tried to get her thoughts together. She had been for a Sunday morning jog, something she rarely did, but the early morning air had been so fresh and Andy had been hanging around the shop, more than anxious to keep an eye on things.

It had been lovely down by the woods and Grace had taken time out to enjoy the sunshine and move her limbs, cramped from spending so long crouched over her workstation.

'Call for you, Grace,' Andy signalled to her as she ran back up the street towards the post house.

'Yes?' she gasped taking the receiver from Andy with a nod of thanks.

'I've got to go to London. I know

Sunday is supposed to be a day of rest, but there's a drama with one of my sister's children so they won't be coming down today after all and, well, it's a long story. What I wondered was would you look after Foxy for me? He likes you and I really don't want to take him to London with me. I'll have my hands full without having to look after a dog who likes to wander.'

'No problem.' Grace's breathing began to return to normal. 'Bring him over. There will be someone here all day.'

'Thanks, Grace. That's another one I owe you.'

Grace waved Daniel off as he headed towards London in his car. 'Right,' she said mock sternly looking down at Foxy who was busy sniffing Amelia's newly washed kitchen floor, 'ground rules.' Grace ticked them off on her fingers. 'No bringing in dirt from the garden. No chasing the hens. No running off into the woods without me. No barking. This is a quiet neighbourhood.' Foxy drummed the floor with his tail. 'If you follow the rules we'll go for a walk after lunch. Now I have to relieve Andy in the shop, so you stay here and keep an eye on things for me. Deal?'

Foxy licked Grace's hand in agreement.

The shop was quiet and Grace took time out to catch up on the world news in the papers, but soon she found her eyelids drooping. There was nothing of interest apart from a political scandal and a minor media star getting up to something or other at an awards ceremony.

Grace glanced at her watch. It was gone two o'clock, a time when she could respectably close up.

Amelia was sitting in a deckchair in the back garden watching Foxy trying to chase a rabbit. Like Grace she had been reading the newspapers and like Grace she seemed to have fallen asleep over them.

She awoke with a start as Grace's shadow temporarily blotted out the sun.

'Goodness, is that the time already? I meant to have lunch on the go.'

'You sit there.' Grace motioned her back in her seat. 'I'm not that hungry and Beattie's out playing bridge, isn't she?'

'Yes, with Clare Jackson, Jason's mother. The pair of them are so much better at it than me so I didn't feel like making up a four.'

'In that case, let's eat our main meal later. I'll get us some fruit and cheese and we'll have a picnic on the grass. Then I'll take Foxy for a walk.'

'Actually,' Amelia said as they tucked into their al fresco meal a little later, 'it was Foxy who started me off.'

Grace looked up from pouring a jug of orange.

'Sorry?'

'When I came downstairs he was fast asleep on the lawn. At first I thought there was something wrong with him. He was so still, but then he saw me and perked up and began to chase a butterfly.'

Grace looked over to where Foxy was

tugging at some grass.

'I'll take him out for a walk. He's left alone a lot of the day. Perhaps he's getting lazy and could do with the exercise.'

'I hope you're not inferring anything by that remark, dear,' Amelia raised a humorous eyebrow. 'I do like my early afternoon snooze too.'

'And you've earned it,' Grace assured her. 'Now is there anything else I can get you?'

'I'll be fine. Off you go for your walk. It'll do you both good.'

The river was over the back of Sycamore House and meandered lazily through the fields. She clambered over a stile and headed down towards the farm. She passed the stables and hearing the sound of horses stamping their hooves inside called Foxy to heel.

'Don't want any trouble,' she said and attached the lead to Foxy's collar. He tugged gamely then accepting the restraint, was content to trot along beside Grace.

Grace waved at one or two of the stable hands and wondered if the owner of the house was still the same crusty old farmer who had chased her and Charlie out of the orchard for scrumping apples. She smiled at the memory.

'We'd better turn back, hadn't we?' she said to Foxy. 'It's uphill and after that jog this morning, my legs are beginning to ache.' Foxy whined. 'Yours, too?' she sympathised. 'You'll have to make the best of it. I can't carry you.'

The walk back was harder going than Grace remembered and by the time she reached the high street she was puffing heavily. Foxy too was reluctant to put his all into the climb and she had been forced to call after him several times as he sat down and showed no intention of moving.

'Come on,' she urged, 'it's not that steep and I made it.'

She felt a tug of guilt as he lapped the water in the old horse trough with an enthusiasm that bordered on greed.

'Sorry,' she apologised, sitting down on the old stone seat. 'I should have thought. You were thirsty, weren't you?' Grace quite fancied a drink of water too, but her thirst would have to wait.

Satiated, Foxy perked up for the final walk along the village street. 'Soon be home,' Grace said trotting along beside him, 'then you can have a really long rest. Andy?' she frowned at the figure loping down the street towards her waving his arms. 'What's the matter?'

'Where've you been?' he demanded. 'I tried ringing your mobile but there was no answer.'

'I didn't take it with me. Andy, what is it?'

'Amelia, Miss MacPherson, she's not well.'

Together they raced towards the shop. 'I found her asleep in the garden. When she didn't answer I raised my voice. She didn't respond.'

'Is her sister back?'

'I telephoned Mrs Jackson's son. He said they were still out at their meeting.

He's coming over, but he hasn't arrived yet.'

'Look after Foxy, will you?' Grace said as she raced through the door.

Amelia looked as though she was still asleep, but to Grace's relief her breathing was steady. Moments later she was joined by Jason.

'Need any help?' he asked, kneeling down beside the deckchair.

'Should we wake her?' Grace asked.

Before he could reply, Amelia awoke with a start.

'Gracious the pair of you did give me a shock,' she put a hand on her heart, 'whatever is it?'

Waves of relief flooded through Grace as she realised Amelia had only been in a heavy sleep.

'Go and tell Andy, will you?' Grace murmured to Jason, 'the poor boy was so worried.'

'Will do.'

'Grace?' Amelia seemed to be her usual sharp self again, 'what's going on?'

'Andy popped round to see you.'

'And he couldn't wake me up?' Amelia's eyes softened at the corners. 'Poor boy. He must have been so worried. Didn't you tell him I always sleep of a Sunday afternoon?'

'Jason is telling him now.'

'I'll make it up to him later. I do apologise, dear. After you left, I didn't feel like moving. It was such a lovely afternoon I nodded off. I didn't sleep very well last night and I suppose it caught up on me.'

'I understand.' Grace squeezed her hand. 'Your rest seems to have done you good. There's colour back in your cheeks.'

'And now I really am rather hungry.'

'In that case I shall start cooking dinner. Beattie should be back soon. Can Jason join us?'

'Of course. Andy too if he wants too, although I suppose his father will wonder where he is.'

To Grace's surprise both Andy and Jason expressed their willingness to join them for their meal.

'My father's taking my mother out this evening,' Andy explained with a shy smile. 'It gets a bit lonely at times watching television on my own.'

'Well,' Jason tossed him a potato peeler, 'as you are staying you can make yourself useful.'

'What am I supposed to do with this?' He looked in surprise at the utensil in his hand.

'When are you off to visit Charlie?' Grace asked Jason as she began hunting for cutlery.

'The day after tomorrow. I'm getting really excited about the deal. Philippe emailed the plans over and I've been studying them.'

'Is it a feasible operation?'

Jason wrinkled his nose. 'Like the curate's egg, it's good in parts, but I've identified a couple of weaknesses.'

'In that case I'm glad they've got you on board. I've seen Charlie go down this route so many times before. He gets fired up with enthusiasm then when things go pear shaped he falls apart.'

'He won't this time.'

'How can you be so sure?'

'Odile's got a good business head on her shoulders. She wants to help out and I think she'll be an asset. I know I've never met her but we've exchanged emails and she seems to be exactly the steadying influence Charlie needs.'

A commotion in the doorway distracted them and soon the kitchen was full of people.

'When I mentioned roast lamb, a couple of the girls invited themselves along,' Beattie explained. 'They've brought some strawberry flan for dessert.'

'Andy,' Jason bawled across the kitchen, 'you'd better have another session with the potato peeler.'

When Jason put his arm around Grace's shoulders at the end of the meal and kissed her ear, before saying, 'that's the best roast lamb dinner I've ever tasted,' his mother sighed.

'What a touching sight.'

'Stop it, Mother,' Jason chided her. 'You're making Andy blush.'

Amelia made everyone jump as she shrieked. 'There's someone at the window.'

'Sorry.' Daniel stumbled into the cramped kitchen. 'I couldn't make myself heard out the front.'

His eyes took in the debris on the table.

'Hello, Daniel, dear,' Amelia waved at him from the far end. 'We would offer you some strawberry flan, but I think Andy's had the last piece.'

'It was mega,' Andy said scooping up the last of the cream with his spoon.

'Bad luck,' Jason sympathised. Then as Daniel's eyes clashed with Grace's, Jason put his arm round her. 'There might be a potato going spare. We've been teaching Andy how to peel them.'

'I don't believe we've been introduced,' Mrs Jackson butted in. 'I'm Jason's mother.'

'Daniel is the new vet, Mother,' Jason explained.

Mrs Jackson widened her eyes. 'So you're the one there was all the fuss about.' She paused. 'Well, I hope things work out for you, but do remember Fieldling doesn't like change.'

'We've only just gone on to electricity,' Jason put in.

Daniel joined in the laughter, but Grace sensed he wasn't pleased to find her virtually in Jason's arms, even if the situation was none of her doing.

'Have you had a good day?' she asked.

'As usual my sister over-reacted. My niece has got a bad head cold, nothing more, thank goodness. The drive back was horrendous. Is that spring water?' he asked eyeing the bottle.

'Help yourself. Andy dear, fetch Daniel a fresh glass and some ice from the freezer. Are you sure I can't tempt you to anything to eat? We've got some cheese and biscuits somewhere, I think,' Amelia said.

'My sister cooked a more than adequate lunch, thank you,' Daniel replied, sipping his drink. 'I really only came round to collect Foxy.'

'I'll find him.' Andy leapt to his feet.

'In that case I'll take your seat,' Daniel slipped into the place vacated by Andy.

Jason kept his arm around Grace's shoulders. 'I hope you're treating my girlfriend well,' he said.

Grace felt herself go as red.

'I didn't know you and Grace were an item,' Daniel said.

'Neither did I,' Mrs Jackson put in, 'but then I never know anything about Jason's girlfriends. If it's any consolation, darling, I approve of this one.' She threw Grace a winning smile. 'It's time my son settled down, don't you think?'

By now Grace was squirming in her seat. If Jason's mother carried on like this she would shortly be demanding they read the banns.

'Footloose and fancy free, that's me,' Grace said in an effort to inject a lighthearted note into the proceedings.

'You like to play the field, do you?'

Daniel queried, his smile not reaching his eyes.

'Why not?' Grace countered.

She noticed Daniel tighten his lips and remembered the kiss down by the lake five years ago. A tiny flame of longing made her stomach feel warm. What was the matter with her?

'Foxy.' Andy's voice broke the spell between them.

'Where was he?' Beattie asked. 'Outside chasing more butterflies?'

'No,' Andy said quietly. 'He's stretched out behind the sofa and,' his voice wobbled, 'I can't wake him up.'

Sycamore House

They buried him under a rhododendron bush in the garden of Sycamore House. Hot tears clogged the back of Grace's throat. Foxy hadn't been playing up, not that day in the woods, when she and the horse riders had discovered him limping or during that afternoon's walk, but no one had realised he wasn't well.

'I think he suffered a stroke,' Daniel said.

'Daniel, I'm so sorry.' Grace was close to sobbing.

'Hey!' He put his arms around her. 'It wasn't your fault.'

'He shouldn't have had a stroke. He was too young and he was in my care. I didn't listen to him.'

'It can happen at any time. In many way dogs are like humans. They get the same illnesses.'

'He died alone while we were all chatting in the kitchen.'

'He would have preferred it that way and his last afternoon was a happy one in Amelia's garden, then going for a walk with you, revisiting all his old haunts.'

Daniel's voice was so soft Grace had to raise her face to his to hear what he was saying. The stubble on his chin scratched her face. She felt the touch of his lips on her hair.

'It wasn't your fault.'

The party had swiftly broken up after Andy's discovery. Grace and Daniel had left everyone clearing up the plates and washing the dishes while they brought Foxy home to Sycamore House. Grace didn't have time to realise this was her first visit to her old home. She was too busy grieving for Foxy.

'He's at peace,' Daniel said softly, 'and it's getting dark. We can't stay out here all night.'

Grace allowed herself to be led indoors. She blinked as Daniel went round turning on lights and closing the curtains. It should have made the house feel cosy, but it didn't.

'Go on through,' he urged, 'you know the way.'

The drawing room was much as she remembered. A huge inglenook fireplace dominated the far side of the room, its centrepiece a selection of dried flowers. To her surprise she saw an easel erected in a far corner. The painting on it was a still life artwork and Grace noted Daniel's initials in the corner.

Not wanting to pry, she sat down on a leather sofa. The coffee table was littered with newspapers, a veterinary gazette and a television guide. This room held so many memories.

Grace inhaled the smell of lavender wax. Years of vigorous dusting had ingrained the polish into the oak features. Her mother's daily had insisted she purchase the best products and it seemed the investment had paid off. Now every surface shone from years of dedicated treatment.

Daniel's carpet was a functional plain

deep blue. Grace remembered her mother had favoured a traditional Turkish weave, a mixture of red, blue, black and white decorated with a Burdock motif.

On a Mediterranean cruise her mother had purchased some Kilim pieces and used them as scatter cushions over their squashy sofa. They helped to disguise all the activity of a family room that bore evidence of dogs — random hair and scratch marks on chair legs and a cat or two snoozing on a window ledge. One of her mother's favourite sayings was, 'If you want to know the best place to sit in a house, look for the cats.'

They loved to curl up in the nook of the fire, which was nearly always lit about four in the afternoon, winter and summer alike, unless it was a really hot day. Grace loved the crackle and smell of the apple logs they used to burn.

She and Charlie would go searching for twigs in the autumn and come home, hot and glowing from their activity and throw them on the fire, watching them burn in the embers while they made a wish. Grace couldn't remember what she had wished for now.

A tear escaped her eye and trickled down her cheek. She wiped it away, annoyed that she had let her emotions get the better of her. Grace had vowed the day she left Sycamore House that she would not live in the past. It was what she had been trying to do for five years.

It had been a mistake to come back, but when Daniel had asked her, and only her to accompany him back to his house, she could hardly refuse.

Jason had been full of sympathy and squeezed her elbow gently. 'If there's anything I can do?' he asked, his blue eyes full of concern.

Daniel had almost yanked her away from him. 'I think you've done enough,' he said in a low voice.

Jason smiled at Daniel. 'In that case I'll help the girls with the washing up. Anyone got a spare apron?' he called out, not in the least chastened by

Daniel's rebuke.

A draught from the doorway brought Grace back to the present.

'I think I would like a coffee,' she said without looking up.

'And that's exactly what Daniel is making,' was the crisp reply.

Grace stiffened as Melissa walked into the room.

'I've only just heard,' she said in a harsh voice she never would have used if Daniel could hear her. 'I passed Jason and his mother in the street. They told me all about it. You have had a busy afternoon, haven't you?'

'You know about Foxy?'

'I do and I seem to recall you gave me a lot of grief for losing him in the woods that day, but at least I didn't kill the poor little chap.'

'Neither did I. Daniel said it was a stroke.'

'He only said that to spare your feelings. Of course it was your fault. Anyone with an ounce of feeling could have seen there was something wrong with him. According to Jason he was limping about the place for days.'

'Then why didn't you notice it when he was in your care?' Grace was stung into retaliating.

Melissa's eyes narrowed. 'Was it all part of a clever plan?'

'I don't understand.' Grace kept her voice steady.

'You've always been jealous of my relationship with Daniel. From the first moment you set eyes on him you didn't want us to get together. What better way to gain his sympathy than to create an emotional bond? And what better way to do that than to grieve together for the loss of a beloved animal?'

'What happened to Foxy was totally unexpected. It was just unfortunate that I happened to be looking after him for the afternoon.'

'In the circumstances I would say I looked after him slightly better than you, don't you agree?' Melissa arched an eyebrow.

'I've done nothing to be ashamed of.'

Grace's head began to throb. She wished Daniel would hurry up with the coffee.

'Apart from worming your way back into your family home,' Melissa snapped. 'That was a smart move and I must admit I didn't see it coming. I might almost have been tempted to try something similar myself, but for my finer feelings.'

Grace could not believe what she was hearing. Melissa was more or less accusing her of sacrificing a dog's life for her own future happiness.

'Not only have you got yourself back in here, you've managed to reinstate yourself at the surgery too. I seriously underestimated your deviousness.'

'Daniel offered me my old job back.'

'Why? It can't have been because of your qualifications can it? So what other method did you use?'

'My local experience.'

'Which you obtained from serving in a shop?'

A noise in the doorway alerted

Melissa to Daniel's presence.

'Let me,' she cooed, leaping to her feet and relieving him of the coffee tray. 'You've had a very trying day, what with your sister's little girl being ill, then that the dreadful drive home through motorway traffic. We won't talk about Foxy.' Her voice was now smooth as treacle. 'Sit down. I'll pour.'

'That's very kind of you,' Daniel said throwing her a grateful smile.

Melissa couldn't resist a catlike gleam in Grace's direction.

'Why don't you sit over there, Grace?' Melissa pointed to one of the armchairs as she joined Daniel on the sofa.

Grace now understood how Daniel must have felt when he saw her and Jason together at the dinner table, virtually glued to the same chair. The raw stab of pain was almost too much to bear.

Melissa moved closer to Daniel and linked her arm in his.

'Tell me all about it.'

'About what?'

'Your day in London of course.' Melissa widened her eyes. 'It's been ages since I've seen you. We need to catch up.'

The coffee was warm and fragrant and it warmed Grace's chilled bones.

'There's not much to tell,' Daniel was talking to Melissa, but Grace could feel his eyes on her.

'How is your dear sister? You must introduce me one day.'

'Grace?' Daniel's questioned her. 'Are you all right?'

'Yes. I'm fine, but I think if you don't mind, I'd like to go home now. Unless you need me for anything?'

'I'm sure we'll manage,' Melissa replied. 'You have an early night. You do look peaky. It's understandable after all you've done today.'

As usual her words had a double meaning, but Daniel didn't seem to notice. He rose to his feet.

'You must let me walk you back,' he insisted.

'No.' That was the last thing Grace wanted. 'You stay here and finish your coffee with Melissa.'

'Caffeine always gives me a restless night,' he replied. 'If you've finished yours, Melissa?'

With an annoyed flash of her deep violet eyes she stood up. 'I could stay until you get back? Why don't I wash up the cups and tidy your kitchen?'

'That won't be necessary, thank you,' Daniel said firmly.

'We could have a nightcap, then?'

'Like Grace I think I want an early night.'

In the face of this remark there was nothing Melissa could do. She searched around for her bag, pretending to have lost it, then her jacket before she was finally ready to leave.

Outside on the pavement she kissed Daniel on the cheek.

'Give me a ring next week and we'll arrange something,' she said.

'Goodnight, Melissa.'

Her keys jangled angrily as she made her way to her car.

'She was only trying to be kind.'

Grace felt duty bound to put in a good word.

'I'm sure.' Daniel sounded convinced, 'but right now Melissa isn't my prime priority. You are.'

By now the light had faded from the day. The only remaining streetlight that worked threw up ghostly patterns on the pavement. In the distance Grace heard an owl in the woods. She had always liked this time of day, but tonight it was giving her the shivers.

'You're cold,' Daniel picked up on her mood.

'Not really.' Grace tried to smile but her face felt too tired.

'Here.' He took off his jacket and draped it around her shoulders. It was warm and smelt of his aftershave and the lemon soap he had used in the kitchen to wash his hands. She clutched it around her body.

'I'm sorry about Melissa,' he said. 'I didn't invite her over. She must have invited herself. She has a habit of doing that.'

'She said she bumped into Jason and his mother. That was how she heard about Foxy.'

'You and Jason,' Daniel began, 'seemed very close this afternoon.'

Grace didn't think she was up to explaining all that had happened. 'Can it wait for another day?'

They were approaching the post office. Grace could see a light on in Amelia's room.

'I don't want to wake everyone up by getting back too late.'

'That has to be about the poorest excuse I've heard in a long time.' There was a smile in Daniel's voice. 'But I'll accept it. You must be bushed. Have a lie in tomorrow,' he insisted. 'I can deal with things.'

'No.' Grace shook her head.

'You are the most obstinate female I have ever met in my life,' he said, 'and you seem to forget I am your boss and correct me if I'm wrong, but don't employees do as their boss says?'

'Monday morning is one of the

busiest times of the week. Besides if I lie around in bed I'll only mope. It's best to keep busy.'

'In that case I'll concede defeat,' Daniel said with a sigh. 'Why is it I always seem to lose out when I try to tell you what to do?'

Grace blinked up at him. She couldn't tell from the expression in his eyes what was going on in his head. She hardly knew what was going on in her own. All she did know was she was experiencing a strong urge for him to kiss her.

A tiny sound escaped her lips as he bent his head towards hers. He almost lifted her out of her shoes as he tightened his arms around her body.

Grace didn't care that they were in full view of anyone who happened to be looking out of their window, or the occasional car that drove by. All she knew was that she didn't want Daniel to stop kissing her. The sensation transported her back five years, when she had been a naïve eighteen-year-old in a pink party dress.

So much had happened to her since, but the sensation of his lips on hers was as wonderful as she remembered it had been.

'Goodnight,' Daniel said in a husky voice as he finally released his hold on her. 'You can keep my coat until tomorrow.'

Without a further word he turned abruptly on his heel and left her standing on the pavement until an insistent tapping behind her attracted her attention.

'Are you going to stand there all night?' Beattie Bishop demanded. 'Now Daniel's stopped kissing you, don't you think it would be a good idea to come inside before you catch your death of cold?'

Melissa Won't Give Up

When Grace had finally snuggled down after a hot bath she realised one of the sisters had placed a hot water bottle in her bed. She cuddled it all night and in the morning her hair was plastered to her head in damp patches and her face was blotchy from the heat.

A tepid bath hadn't helped to cool her temperature. Early June was not the month for hot water bottles, but Grace appreciated the gesture and thanked Amelia over a hurried breakfast.

'You're going in today?' she sounded surprised.

'Of course.' Grace gulped down her tea and a couple of mouthfuls of cereal, which she only ate to please Amelia. Her stomach was still churning and she didn't know when it would get back to normal.

The thought of facing Daniel made

her head spin. She hadn't been certain but last night as he released her, she thought she caught a glimpse of a racy convertible easing past them with Melissa at the wheel.

'I nearly forgot to tell you,' Amelia turned back from the fridge. 'Charlie telephoned last night. He said to tell you he's coming over for a short business visit. Then Jason is going back with him to France.'

'When?'

'Next week. They are going to stay with Jason's mother. Odile is coming too. I am looking forward to meeting her.'

'I thought Jason was going out there first.'

'I believe there's been a change of plan, but you'll have to discuss it with Charlie, dear. My hearing's not all it should be and I tend to get confused on the telephone. He's going to call back this evening.'

The thought of seeing Charlie again cheered Grace up and there was a smile on her face as she pushed open the surgery door.

There wasn't time for a private word with Daniel before the first of the day's appointments arrived, to be followed by a constant stream of visitors.

One or two knowing glances were cast in her direction and Grace had the suspicion that word had got round the village that last night she had been seen kissing Daniel Stafford under a streetlight. By the end of the day she fully expected her reputation to be in tatters.

Most people seemed to have heard about Foxy and Grace received many condolences on Daniel's loss, along with a few offers of a replacement puppy, which she politely declined.

Grace bit down a gesture of annoyance as the telephone rang early afternoon. Daniel had been called out and during his absence Grace had snatched up the chance to have a quick break.

'Hello?' she mumbled through a mouthful of sandwich.

'Hi, sis.'

'Charlie.' She hurried swallowed her sandwich.

'Eating on the job?' he teased. 'What will Daniel have to say about that?'

'It's my lunch.'

'Sorry, didn't realise it was your meal break. It's gone half past three here.'

'We're an hour behind you and it's been a hectic morning.'

'I rang Miss MacPherson last night. Do you know she said I could call her Amelia now? I think we've finally been accepted back into the fold. Anyway, as you were out I said I'd call back.'

'She gave me your message. When can I expect the pleasure of your company?'

'Hopefully some time next week. Do you think you can get any time off?'

'I'm not sure. The surgery has only recently reopened and things are very busy. I think half the population of Fieldling possesses a sick animal. I hardly have a moment to myself.'

'Daniel Stafford doesn't appreciate

you. I hope you wangled yourself a huge great rise.'

'I did.'

'And a company car?'

Grace laughed. 'Well, I didn't get the car.'

'Keep trying,' Charlie advised her. 'So why the big change of heart over the job?'

'Mine or Daniel's?'

'Both of you really. I thought you walked out on him and he was looking for a mega professional model type with qualifications as long as your arm.'

'Let's say I persuaded him he couldn't do without me.'

'Nice one,' Charlie sounded impressed. 'Any more trouble from Dr Malcolm?'

Grace had almost forgotten the incident that had sparked off the reason for her original resignation from the surgery.

'No, and I don't think we will.'

'Why's that?'

'His son, Andy, has started working at the shop, so we're all the best of friends now. I bumped into his father the other day and he was almost polite to me.'

'Daniel still doesn't know it was me and not you who parked in the doc's reserved place?'

'I haven't told him and it's old news now. So much has happened since.'

'All the same I think Daniel should be told. I don't like hiding behind my big sister's apron strings.'

'Leave it, Charlie.'

'Anything you say, but if you have a change of heart I'm prepared to own up.'

A light began to flash on the switchboard in front of Grace, indicating an incoming call. 'I'm going to have to go,' she said.

'What's all this about you and JJ dating?'

'My relationship with Jason Jackson is my affair. Look, I really must go. Daniel's out and I've a call waiting.'

'Bye then, darling,' Charlie bellowed.

A shadow appeared in front of Grace's desk.

'Surgery?' Daniel answered the call on the second line.

Grace dropped the receiver back into its cradle.

'I didn't know you were back,' she mouthed at him.

He finished his call before scribbling an appointment on the pad in front of him.

'Another emergency,' he said, 'and it's just as well I came in the back way, isn't it?'

'I was only . . . '

'The lines are not to be used for personal calls. You do have a mobile, don't you?'

'Yes.'

'Then use it to speak to your boyfriends.'

There was no trace of the compassionate gentleman of the previous evening. The old Daniel was glaring back at her and he looked in no mood to compromise.

'If you'd let me explain,' Grace began.

'There isn't time. In case you hadn't noticed there are several more callers in the queue to be answered. I have to go out again. While I'm gone please don't clog the line with personal calls especially ones of an intimate nature.'

Robbed of speech, Grace felt as though she had been punched in the stomach. The call from Charlie was the first personal one she had ever taken in the office since Daniel had taken over and it was supposed to have been during her meal break when there were no clients in the waiting room.

She flicked the line on the switchboard not bothering to tell Daniel he had left his bag behind on her desk. Grace experienced a guilty if vicarious thrill of satisfaction a few moments later when there was an angry draught of air from the door as Daniel strode back in to pick it up. Quelling the childish urge to make a face at his retreating back, she turned her attention to the next call.

It was seven o'clock before Grace

finished writing up her day's notes. Daniel still hadn't returned to the surgery and she wondered if perhaps he had gone straight home after his call out. It was unusual for home visits to take so long and she hoped it was nothing serious.

If it had been she supposed he would have put a call through to her, unless he was still annoyed over what he saw as her unprofessional behaviour, even so she wouldn't have thought he would let that influence the business side of things.

Grace massaged her aching neck. She was tired. It would be nice to have a day off when Charlie visited, but there was no way she was going to ask any favours of Daniel Stafford. He clearly didn't trust her to behave in a professional manner in his absence and she really didn't want to lose her job for a second time.

'Trying to earn brownie points?' a voice behind her enquired.

Annoyed with herself for not locking

the door earlier, Grace turned to face Melissa.

'Daniel won't thank you for it,' she taunted, 'that's if you're still trying to curry favour with him after being responsible for Foxy's death.'

'What are you talking about now, Melissa?' Grace asked with a weary sigh.

'You and Daniel.'

'Whatever there is between us is nothing to do with you.'

'Even though you advertise your affair by kissing him in full view of the village? Hardly the way to keep things quiet, is it? And don't deny it. I saw you with my own eyes.'

'So it was you who drove past us?'

'I don't know what you're doing, Grace, but it won't work.'

'I'm not playing any game. Daniel walked me home that was all.'

'Do you know where he is now?'

'No.'

'Well, I do.'

Grace frowned at her. The reason for

Melissa's visit wasn't clear, but she had no doubt it wasn't without purpose.

'He had a puncture and I happened to be driving by so I gave him a lift to the garage. He is there now sorting out his tyre. When he's through we're off to have dinner together. I saw the light was still on in the surgery as I was driving past so I dropped in to tell you there's no point in waiting around for him. If you've got any messages I can pass them on.'

'That won't be necessary,' Grace clipped back at her, 'thank you.'

She began tidying her desk.

'Yes, well, I can't hang around any longer either. I've had a busy day too and,' she added with a knowing smile, 'it's not over yet.'

'Have a good evening,' Grace said as she locked her work away in a drawer.

'I intend to,' Melissa called over her shoulder.

Not looking where she was going she bumped into another visitor standing in the doorway.

'Steady,' Jason laughed, sidestepping the impact. 'Goodness, you're looking vicious. Has something upset your apple cart?'

'Not at all,' Melissa smiled sweetly at him. 'I'm off to have dinner with Daniel Stafford.'

'And you've been crowing over Grace, is that it?'

'Certainly not.'

'Melissa, you are so easy to see through, you shouldn't even bother trying to fib. Besides, Grace and I have a date for this evening, so if you've been trying to stir things up, you really have been wasting your time.'

Grace watched the exchange open mouthed with surprise. This was the first she knew about any date with Jason.

'So are you. I saw Grace and Daniel kissing under a lamp post last night.'

'That sounds very Parisian,' Jason said with a teasing note in his voice.

'I'm serious.'

'In that case should you be going out

with Daniel tonight? You clearly suspect him and Grace of being an item.'

Melissa tossed her head. 'They are not.'

'Now you're in danger of contradicting yourself I'd say, wouldn't you?'

Narrowing her eyes until they resembled that of a cat's, Melissa threw him a contemptuous glance before sweeping out of the surgery.

'You shouldn't make fun of her like that.' Grace couldn't help laughing at the gloating expression on Jason's face.

'I can't help it. At times she is so outrageous she deserves to be taken down a peg or two.'

'What was all that about us having dinner together?'

'I actually said we only had a date, but now you come to mention it, do you fancy something Italian at the wine bar in town? I could murder some linguini.'

'I would need to go home and change first.'

'You look fine to me.'

'In my work overall?'

'Tell you what, why don't I charm Amelia and Beattie while you freshen up? Then we can go straight on.'

'Is there any special reason for this celebration?'

'There is indeed.' Jason beamed at her. 'I have just been told by my solicitor that the final contract is ready for my signature and when Charlie comes over to visit he can countersign it. We are then in a go situation.'

'You mean, the business?'

'I do. We are almost up and running. So can you think of a better reason not to celebrate?'

'Jason, that's wonderful news.'

Grace flung her arms around him. As he lifted her up in the air and gave her a bear hug squeeze, Daniel strode through the surgery door.

A Surprise At The Ball

'It's all right for you,' Grace grumbled, as Odile stood behind her, pencil slim and effortlessly elegant. She frowned at her reflection in Amelia's wardrobe mirror. 'You'd look stunning wearing a bin liner.'

'Cherie?' Odile frowned her thoughts elsewhere. 'The light in this room, it is too dark.'

'How can a light be dark?' Grace teased.

'We need peach wallpaper, soft carpets, gentle music, an ambience of tranquillity.'

Grace's grumble turned into a full-blown grin that stretched across her face.

'Getaway.' She nudged Odile.

'What is this getaway?' Odile raised her perfectly plucked eyebrows.

'Amelia MacPherson doesn't do

ambiance and may I remind you we are only in her bedroom because she very kindly gave us permission to use her full length mirror. I don't have one.'

'The English.' Odile shook her head as is she would never understand the race. 'You do not have what every French woman considers essential.'

'Let's not go into all that.' Grace stared back at her reflection. 'What I need is something to make me look as chic and sophisticated as you. It isn't that much of a challenge is it?' she asked, her spirits plummeting as Odile looked daunted by the task.

'First we must style your hair. I have spoken to the coiffeuse in the village, but I don't think she understood the effect I was looking for, so we will do it ourselves. I will trust this Doris with the cutting but no more,' Odile said with a stern frown.

Grace opened her mouth to explain Doris was a dab hand at shampoo and sets, but anything else was outside her sphere of expertise, but Odile was not in the mood for interruption.

'Now, the make-up. I think less is more.'

'What?'

'You have the beautiful English complexion, but you do not look after it. Soon you will have the feet of the birds around your eyes.'

'Crows' feet to you too,' Grace retaliated.

'You think I am joking?' Odile widened her brown eyes. 'Beauty is a very serious matter.'

'Perhaps giving me a make-over is a mistake.' It was Grace who now began to feel daunted. 'The charity ball is tomorrow night. We can't work miracles.'

Clare Jackson, Jason's mother, had bamboozled Charlie and Odile into buying tickets for the social event of the summer. In her position as charity chair she was not a lady to be argued with.

'It is for a very good cause,' she insisted, 'and it will raise your business profile, Charlie.'

Odile immediately saw the sense in

that suggestion and agreed with her.

'As Jason's partner for the evening,' Clare Jackson turned her attention to Grace, 'you will of course be sitting at the top table.'

After Grace had recovered from the shock, she began to panic. She had only called by to see if Charlie and Odile fancied meeting up later.

'Sorry.' Jason made a face at her as soon as his mother was out of earshot. 'I gave Mum the impression we are an item. She much prefers you to Melissa and I think she's worried Melissa will shoehorn her way onto the top table and take charge.' He lowered his voice. 'They don't get on.'

'I gathered that.'

'And I don't want to get landed with one of my mother's friend's horsey daughters. I mean they are nice girls, but a little too hearty for my taste.'

'So you told your mother you had invited me to partner you?'

'You will help me out, won't you? I'll make it up to you. I promise.'

'Dinner at Romeo's?'

'Not one I've heard of. Where is it?'

'It's in France, my mother's local, actually. It has been awarded goodness knows how many gold stars and dinner there costs an arm and a leg.'

'Then it will be my pleasure to treat you,' Jason replied with a gallant bow.

'You always were a gentleman,' Grace laughed, 'and I won't hold you to it.'

'Please do,' Jason insisted without a trace of sarcasm.

Grace sighed. She really liked Jason and hoped Odile would be able to fix him up with one of her friends, when he moved out to France. He deserved a nice girlfriend, one that wouldn't take advantage of his easy going nature and natural generosity.

'We will need a light foundation to tone down your freckles, some bronze blusher and a pale pink lipstick, with a suggestion of mascara. Yes,' Odile nodded. 'That will be perfect. Now the dress.'

She stood with her hands on her hips

and looked Grace up and down.

Odile reminded Grace a little of the pictures she had seen of General de Gaulle when he was disagreeing with his English counterparts. There was no budging her. She was going to have her way.

'We must go shopping.'

Meekly obeying orders, Grace allowed herself to be driven into town where she and Odile indulged in an flurry of retail therapy that made Grace's eyes water.

'Jason has insisted I buy you something for helping him out with his problem.'

'He was only being polite.' Grace looked down at the vast quantity of expensive carriers bags they were carrying, 'and I don't think he intended helping out quite this much.'

'Nonetheless, his mother will expect you to look the part.'

That was the punchline and Odile knew it and ruthlessly played it for all it was worth. Odile and Clare Jackson had taken to each other from the moment they first met. Odile was such a lovely girl she bonded with everyone and Grace could understand why Charlie was mad about her.

'If she wasn't spoken for,' Jason confided to Grace after they had been introduced, 'I might be tempted to make a play for her. She is going to make the charity ball buzz.'

Now with her hair freshly lowlighted and swept up in an elegant pleat, Grace hardly recognised her reflection. The long turquoise dress she wore was perfectly plain, apart from the huge bow at the back. Odile had pounced on the cobweb lace shawl her mother had given Grace for her birthday and draped it around her shoulders.

'Perfect. Now you shall go to the ball, Cinderella,' Odile said as she finished making the final adjustments to Grace's hair.

'Don't you look lovely, dear?' Amelia's eyes almost came out on stalks as she popped her head round the bedroom door. 'I wouldn't have realised it was you. Quite the young lady.'

'It's all down to Odile,' Grace insisted.

Odile was looking effortlessly chic in a geometric black and white print mini dress. The only other colour in her ensemble was her red clutch bag.

'Charlie and Jason have arrived. They're downstairs talking to Beattie. The taxi has been booked for half-past seven.'

'Time for a glass of champagne first, I think then,' Odile insisted.

'Good heavens,' Amelia fluttered. 'Wherever did you get that idea? I, er, don't think we've actually got any. There's not much call for that sort of thing in the shop.'

'A bottle has been cooling in your fridge ever since we returned from our shopping expedition. Come.' Odile clicked her fingers at them.

Amelia and Grace trailed after Odile, slightly in awe of her organisational qualities.

Jason and Charlie leapt to their feet as Odile swept into the room carrying her champagne. Amelia and Grace followed with the glasses on a tray.

'Sis?' Charlie gaped, 'that is you?'

'Hardly a flattering response,' Odile delivered a stern glance in his direction.

'She's not, I mean, wow.' Charlie's face now lit up in devilment. 'That should knock Daniel Stafford into the next century.'

'Jason, uncork the bottle please,' Odile began organising a table on which to place the glasses, 'and Charlie stop making silly comments and come and help, please.'

Both men leapt to her command.

'At the risk of incurring Melissa's wrath,' Jason murmured in Grace's ear, 'I'd like to endorse Charlie's flattery. You do look wonderful. Sure you're not on the lookout for a beau?'

'If I was you'd be my first choice.' Grace found herself in the unusual situation of enjoying being the centre of attention.

She had never seen Jason in dinner dress before, but in his immaculate white shirt, black bow tie and dinner jacket she realised exactly how handsome he was.

'As we're exchanging compliments, you look terrific too.' Grace wrinkled her nose as the champagne bubbles tickled her nostrils.

'You know Daniel is Melissa's date for the evening, don't you?' Jason asked in a quiet voice.

'She made sure I knew.'

Charlie proposing a toast interrupted Grace's reply.

'To our lovely ladies, Odile and Grace.'

'Don't forget us,' Amelia MacPherson tittered.

She and her sister were wearing almost identical crushed velvet dresses that had been hanging on the line all afternoon in the hope that the fresh air would rid them of the smell of mothballs.

Odile had very kindly said they looked lovely and with their faces now flushed from the champagne, Grace felt a surge of affection for the two ladies who had shown her nothing but kindness when her friends in the village were few and far between.

'Amelia and Beattie.' Grace was the first to raise her glass. The others followed her example.

'Taxi's here,' Charlie called out as car lights flashed through the curtains. 'Everyone ready?'

'Darling, where have you been?' Clare Jackson floated down the steps of the country club to greet her son.

Jason gave her a kiss. 'Are we late?'

'Most of the VIPs are here. They're in the marquee. Thank goodness it's a fine night. I don't know what we would have done had it been raining. Grace?' Her voice rose in surprise as she took in her appearance, 'what a lovely dress. Come and give me a kiss.'

'I hope I look all right?' Grace asked, experiencing a pang of nerves.

'Thank you, my dear,' Clare's voice was husky, 'for looking after my Jason. I know you're not really an item so it was very kind of you to take him on for the evening. I do hope you have a good time.'

The two women smiled at each other in complete understanding.

'I'm sure I will,' Grace replied.

'Now we had better get going,' Clare said. 'The action is this way.'

The little group made its way towards the music emanating from the marquee.

'What's the order of play?' Jason asked.

'Mingle for a bit I think, then we'll have dinner before we start the fund-raising activities.'

Soon mutual friends, all eager to be introduced to Charlie's beautiful fiancée, surrounded their party. In the ensuing crush Grace became separated from Jason. Amelia and Beattie's bridge friends were threatening to de-camp to the house to set up card tables to get away from all the noise and Grace found herself on her own.

'You look different.'

She didn't have to turn round to know it was Daniel.

Ever since his date with Melissa after

his puncture, their relationship had reverted to that of business colleagues. After Daniel had discovered her and Jason together in the surgery, there had been no more shared intimacies between them for which Grace was pleased.

Quite how it had happened she didn't know, but she would be fooling herself if she didn't accept the inevitable. She had fallen in love with Daniel Stafford. She seriously suspected she had been in love with him for years, but her subconscious had blocked her mind to the possibility.

Despite all he had said he and Melissa were back together and she had no wish to be accused for a second time of breaking up their relationship.

Taking a deep breath Grace raised her chin before greeting him.

'Daniel.' She smiled into his hazel eyes and tried not to gulp with shock.

She had thought Jason and Charlie looked good in their evening suits, but Daniel outclassed them both. His outdoor tan looked even healthier against the pristine white of his shirt, which fitted him like a glove. His broad shoulders stretched against the fabric of his jacket and Grace did her best to ignore the flame of longing which leapt up inside her as she looked into his face.

'There you are.'

For the first time ever Grace welcomed Melissa's intrusion.

'Good grief.' The almond eyes narrowed. 'Haven't you rather gone over the top, Grace? I mean this is only the local charity we are talking about.'

'I'm on the top table, with Jason and his mother,' Grace explained, glad her voice wasn't shaking.

'Yes, I had heard.' Melissa's voice was about as warm as a glacier.

'What table are you on?' she asked.

'We're down by the fire exit,' Daniel explained with the ghost of a smile.

'Only because you weren't sure you were coming.' It was all Melissa could do not to hiss.

'We got a last minute cancellation,' Daniel said. 'As we're by the fire exit I'll be able to make a quick getaway if the evening drags on, and from the way things are shaping up it looks like it could be a long night. I had an early start today and they ruin your social life.'

If looks could kill then Grace decided Daniel would now be flat on his back. Before she had a chance to commiserate, a whining noise from the microphone preceded Clare's announcement that dinner was about to be served.

Jason's mother was in her element as she announced the first of the evening's fundraisers.

'We are pleased to have with us tonight Odile Risset, Charlie Maxwell's beautiful French fiancée.'

There were several cheers and whistles, mainly from the males present as Odile stood up acknowledging the applause and blowing kisses at everyone.

'Earlier in the evening Odile volunteered to perform the French classic, *No Regrets* if everyone present promised to donate a little something to the charity fund. I am pleased to say everyone has, so I now have the pleasure of introducing Odile Risset who will be joined on stage by her future sister-in-law Grace Maxwell. I am sure Grace needs no introduction to most of you. She is of course our very efficient vet's assistant and my son Jason's current partner.'

If the mayor had suddenly decided to conga around the marquee, Grace could not have been more surprised.

'The wine's gone to your mother's head, Jason,' she hissed. 'I promised no such thing. For heaven's sake,' she pleaded, 'get me out of this.'

'Coward,' Jason taunted.

'You owe me one.'

'Get up there on the stage. These people have paid good money to hear you and I should warn you they could turn very angry if you disappoint them. Don't they still use the guillotine in France?' he teased.

'I can't sing.'

'I don't think this lot are expecting an operatic performance. They'll probably join in when you're half way through so don't worry about it.'

Odile was now standing by Grace's chair and one or two of the more boisterous element amongst the diners began banging the tablecloths with their spoons, demanding to know why they were being kept waiting.

'Allez,' Odile urged, going into General de Gaulle mode again.

On shaking legs Grace stood up. In a far corner of the room she saw Daniel. Her eyes clashed with his. Something of the old Grace resurfaced. In her prime she would have met the challenge without a second thought. It was the taunting expression on Melissa's face that goaded her into action.

She grabbed the microphone from Clare.

'Are you all absolutely sure about this?' she asked.

Her query was met with a robust response.

'In that case,' she grinned, 'you've asked for it.'

With legs still on the wobbly side Grace followed Odile onto the stage as the strains of the famous song began to drift into the room. Odile started first and as she gained confidence Grace joined in, empathising with the words.

She had done a lot of things in her life and she had no reason to regret any of them. She gave the song her best and the audience joined in. As the two girls reached their finale nearly everyone was standing up and cheering.

The two girls embraced and Grace murmured in Odile's ear, 'if you ever do anything like that to me again I may not be responsible for my actions.'

'Cherie,' Odile reminded Grace of the Little Sparrow herself, 'there will be no more need of my simple therapy. Today you have made closure on your past. It is time to move forward and if Daniel Stafford has not fallen in love with you tonight, then I fear he never will.'

The Truth Is Spoken

'That was quite some performance,' Daniel barred Grace's way as she emerged from the cloakroom.

After her duet with Odile she had been in desperate need of a freshen up. Most of Odile's beautifully applied make-up had run and an urgent repair job was needed. People had gathered round to congratulate her, including Clare Jackson who was happy to report that the evening had been an unmitigated success and donations had far exceeded expectations.

'And most of it is down to you and Odile,' she gushed as they occupied adjacent padded stools in front of the mirrors to re-apply their make-up.

'Nonsense.' Grace began to feel embarrassed.

'You should have seen everyone belting the words out with you. I'm surprised the marquee didn't blow away. It was a stroke of genius Odile suggesting we roll down the words behind you. She wrote them all out for us in huge great letters.

'She's such a thoughtful girl, isn't she? Her actions turned the thing into a very vibrant singalong. You've quite cemented Anglo-French relations tonight, my dear. I can't wait for our twinning visit next summer. I'm assuming I can count on your support?'

'Er, I'd have to take a rain check on that one.'

'I've no idea what that expression means,' Clare patted her hand, 'so I'll take it as a yes. Now I'd better go and mingle.' Clare was still beaming. 'There are one or two more donors I need to charm into making donations and as everyone is in such a good mood I'm hoping for a generous response.'

'Good luck,' Grace said as she began to re-apply her mascara. 'I think I'll put my feet up.'

'You've done your bit, dear. Enjoy

the rest of your evening. By the way,' Clare said with a mischievous twinkle in her eye, 'there were some who weren't too happy about your performance. It was far too, shall we say engaging?'

Grace's heart sank.

'Naming no names of course.' Mrs Jackson touched the side of her nose in a gesture of silence.

Grace didn't need to be told. She knew. She had scored where Melissa had failed. It wasn't a position she relished, or one of her own making, but Melissa would not see it like that and now Daniel was standing in the foyer of the clubhouse insisting she join him for a dance in the marquee.

'You can't refuse me,' he insisted, 'I'm your boss.'

'Where's Melissa?'

'Dancing with Jason. Come on.'

Hand in hand with Daniel they made their way across the lawn and back into the marquee.

'It's a bit of a squash,' Grace said as

Daniel drew her into his arms.

'That gives me a good excuse to hold you close then, doesn't it? Listen, they're playing our tune.'

'We don't have one.'

'I know but I thought I'd give it a go,' he teased her. 'I was half hoping you'd put your head on my shoulder.'

'Daniel, this has to stop.'

'Why?'

'You know why.'

'I don't actually. Why don't you tell me?'

As they moved in time to the music, Grace wasn't sure exactly why. She could smell the masculine aroma of his after-shave and it was addling her thoughts. She couldn't think straight.

'In case you hadn't noticed the music's finished,' Daniel murmured in her ear. 'I mean I would be quite happy to carry on shuffling around with you, but we appear to be the only two people still trying to dance and people are looking at us.'

'What?' Grace drew out of his arms,

flushed and embarrassed.

'I wouldn't mention it only the musicians have gone for their break, and I rather think we're in the way.'

Good-natured guests walked round them, one or two with knowing smiles on their faces.

'I think I need some fresh air,' Grace stumbled towards the tent flaps.

'I know, let's go down to the lake.'

Grace didn't have the strength to argue with his decision. The night was cool and they weren't the only guests enjoying the air on the lawn.

'I'd say from the number of enthusiastic conversations going on, the event has been a roaring success, wouldn't you?'

Daniel linked fingers with Grace.

'There's no need to pull back,' he said, 'I only want to make sure you don't twist your ankle. Some parts of the lawn are a bit dodgy and those shoes are more suited for dancing than walking, aren't they? Lovely dress, by the way.'

'Odile chose it.'

'She's quite a girl, isn't she? I've never met her before.'

'You've spoken to her?'

Grace hadn't told Odile much about Daniel. With her innate sense of sophistication, it would not have taken her two minutes to work out the chemistry between Grace and her boss, as it was she seemed to have accurately summed up the situation.

'Yes, she was telling me about Charlie and Jason's business venture. She's got a good head on her shoulders. Let's hope she's the making of Charlie and that this will be the end to his silly schemes.'

A faint breeze blew off the lake.

'Would you like to sit down?' Daniel asked.

'I think we should be getting back. Now the music has finished Melissa will be looking for you.'

'Then let her look.'

Grace blinked, not sure she had heard Daniel correctly.

'At the risk of sounding ungallant, Melissa sort of forced this date on me. I wouldn't have accepted her invitation, only she told me you were going with Jason. So I agreed to be her escort for the evening.'

'Why should it matter to you who I was going with?' Grace asked.

'Because I was going to ask you to accompany me.'

'You were?' A lump lodged in Grace's chest making it difficult for her to speak.

'Grace,' he put a hand to her face. 'I've got to tell you how I really feel about you.'

'No.' She flinched.

'Don't you feel the same way about me?'

'It's not that. I mean, yes, no, I don't know. Why does everything seem to happen to us down by this lake?'

'It is rather like an action replay, isn't it?'

Daniel drew her into his arms. Grace no longer had the strength to struggle.

It was heady stuff looking into his hazel eyes.

'Why are you doing this?' she managed to ask. 'I mean you don't even like me.'

'Whatever gave you that idea?'

'You did. You're always picking holes in what I do and you fired me because I wasn't qualified enough for the job I had been doing for years.'

'Actually you fired yourself, but you're right, I probably would have asked you to leave.'

'My case is proven then.'

'Only because I didn't think it was quite ethical for the vet to be in a relationship with his assistant.'

'What sort of relationship?'

'A personal one and once the village got hold of the news, we would have had no chance of keeping things quiet. I thought your reputation didn't deserve any more knocks. Didn't you wonder why I was always picking on you?'

'Frequently.'

'I was hoping you would resign.

Legislation being what it is these days, it's very difficult to dismiss anyone.'

'If you felt like that why did you offer me my job back?'

'A moment of weakness. When I saw you were reduced to serving in the shop . . . '

'I like doing it and the MacPherson sisters were wonderful to me when no-one else was.'

'I know, but Andy took over some of your duties and then, well, you weren't having any success looking for employment.'

'Don't you dare say you took pity on me.'

'I wouldn't dream of it,' Daniel said mildly.

'I can look after myself.'

'Grace, you have nothing left to prove. Whatever debt you feel your father left to society, you have more than repaid.'

'Have I?' she asked in a shaky voice.

'You have. Now, you and me.'

'What about Melissa?'

'Let's leave her out of this.'

'Are you using her?'

'I have given her no encouragement, but she can be very possessive. Tell me, didn't you sense something between us when I kissed you on this very spot five years ago?'

'No.' Grace did her best to deny her feelings.

'Well I did. Would you like me to remind you what it was like?'

'Daniel, please,' Grace implored. 'Melissa saw us kissing under the lamp post the night Foxy died. So did Beattie Bishop.'

'I expect there were a lot more witnesses, but we won't go into all that now. I'd never really believed in love at first sight, but from the first moment we met I don't think there was any other girl for me.'

'For five years?'

'I'll admit I went on the odd date of course, but you were always at the back of my mind.'

'I was a spoilt brat.'

'I saw underneath all that and you have proved otherwise.'

Daniel put up a hand and tucked a stray curl behind her ear.

'There, a running repair. Don't know how long it will last.'

He groaned.

'What's the matter?' Grace stiffened.

'Melissa's heading this way. Shall we share another kiss? It worked last time.'

Grace was unable to struggle as Daniel lowered his face to hers.

'I might have known.' Melissa's voice woke the snoozing ducks and they began to quack in consternation. They paddled around in circles, creating ripples on the lake.

'This is getting to be a habit,' Daniel said raising his face. 'Is there anything I can do for you, Melissa?'

'You can stop kissing Grace for a start.'

'We hadn't actually got that far.'

Grace tried to wriggle out of his hold, but Daniel's hands were clenched firmly to her upper arms.

'Don't you realise no man is safe when she's around? I've left a distraught Jason in the club looking for her. His mother too is very disappointed in her behaviour.'

'At the risk of sounding rude, that's balderdash,' Daniel replied. 'But let's not get undignified about things.'

'Is that all everyone can do all evening? Discuss my feelings?' Grace elbowed her way into the verbal exchange.

'I took time out to join in a very rousing chorus of *No Regrets*,' Daniel insisted. 'Best singing I've ever done even though my French is a bit rusty, but I don't think anyone noticed. They were too busy bawling out their own version of the song.'

'Let go of me.' Grace struggled to free herself from Daniel's hold. 'I suggest you sort things out with Melissa. I played the victim last time. I'm not going to do it again.'

'Thought I heard raised voices, sis. Anything wrong?'

'Charlie? Take me home,' Grace pleaded.

'The evening's not over yet.'

'I want to go home.'

'But no.' Odile had now joined them with Jason bringing up the rear. 'Jason I told you to dance with Melissa. Why did you not do as I said?'

'I did,' Jason protested, 'but the music finished and I couldn't physically detain her, could I? I mean manners and all that. Besides she saw Daniel and Grace heading for the lake and she was off like a greyhound following the rabbit.'

'What is this rabbit?' Odile demanded.

'He'll explain another time,' Charlie said. 'Jason, do me a favour. Take Grace home for me.'

'My pleasure.' He held out his arm.

'I need to have a word with Daniel.'

Charlie watched Jason escort his sister across the lawn. Taking advantage of his and Daniel's inattention, Melissa linked arms with Daniel then faced Charlie.

'If you're going to plead for your sister's honour, then don't bother,' she said.

'What I've got to say won't take long,' Charlie said carefully, ignoring her and addressing Daniel.

'Where I come from,' Odile addressed Melissa, 'we have more pride than to cling onto a man who isn't interested in us.'

Daniel removed Melissa's arm from his and turned to talk to Charlie.

'I had no wish to upset your sister, Charlie. I hope you believe me.'

'It's none of my affair,' Charlie insisted, 'but I can't have you thinking she was responsible for the incident in the doctor's reserved parking space.'

'The what?'

'It was me. She took the blame because it was her car and she knew I didn't have the money to pay her fine. Over the years I've been a drain on my sister and now my fortunes are looking up, I intend to pay every debt I owe her. It can't have been easy for her when our father died.

'Our mother was very dependant on her until she re-married, and as for me, well, I took off. I absolved a lot of the responsibility that as the son of the house should have been mine. I'm not proud of my behaviour, but I'm making a clean start of things. Grace took on two jobs because I wasn't pulling my weight. I just thought you ought to know.'

'Thanks for telling me, Charlie.' He and Daniel shook hands. 'I suspected something like that was the case. I hope you'll now believe me when I say there really is nothing to my relationship with Melissa apart from that of good friends and I'm not playing fast and loose with your sister's affections.'

'I'm pleased to hear it,' Charlie replied. 'We'll take our leave of you, then.'

The two men glanced across to where Odile was still confronting Melissa.

'My future sister-in-law is a lovely woman,' Odile said. 'She loves Daniel and he loves her. You have to let him go,' she added in a softer voice.

'What do you know about love?'

'I love Charlie and one day you'll find someone.'

'I moved back here to get over a broken engagement. I thought fate was playing into my hands when I bumped into Daniel. He was an old boyfriend.'

'Then he should remain that way. Come, I think we should be friends.'

'You do?' Melissa looked at Odile in disbelief.

'Of course. In time you will be friends again with Grace too, won't you?'

'I don't know about that.'

'You have to because, you see, I intend asking Grace to be my bridesmaid when I get married and of course I would expect you as a beauty therapist to be involved in doing the make-up and the hair. I will not have the time.'

'You want me to be your consultant?'

'Yes.'

'I don't know what to say,' Melissa gasped.

'I hope it will be yes. It will be a big wedding. There will be lots of people and a party afterwards. I will invite all my French men friends to attend and I will tell them about you. Jean-Claud, now he likes English girls, so too does Pierre.'

'Glad to see the girls are making a go of it,' Charlie said as he watched Odile and Melissa engage in animated conversation. He smiled at Daniel. 'By the way, if you really are thinking of getting together with Grace, there's something you ought to know about her and I speak from a brother's experience.'

'More confessions?' Daniel queried.

'I love my sister very much, but I'm the first to admit she can be a bit tricky at times. She is immensely stubborn and has more than her fair share of family pride so you may have a challenge on your hands when you try to get back into her good books. If I were you, I'd leave it a day or two before well, you know, saying anything.'

'You don't mind?' Daniel asked carefully, 'about the two of us?'

'I'd be delighted if you can pull it off.

You're so right for each other, but it's Grace you've got to convince, not me. Actually you might have a bit of a problem with my mother too, now I come to think about it, but she'll come round once she learns you're not as bad as you've been painted.'

'I'm pleased to hear it,' Daniel said with a look of relief. 'Anything else I should know?'

'Only that I'd welcome you as a brother-in-law. Go for it, but wear a tin hat,' Charlie joked.

'I'll take your advice on board,' Daniel laughed with him.

'Let's all go back to the party,' Odile called over. 'I'm sure I saw an unopened bottle of champagne in one of the buckets.'

'Good idea,' Charlie agreed. 'I don't know about anyone else but I really could do with a long cool drink.'

The four of them headed towards the music as it started up again in the marquee.

A New Beginning

'Grace, dear.' Amelia MacPherson poked her head round her bedroom door. 'Are you awake?'

Grace grunted from under the bedclothes.

'I am sorry to disturb you, but there's a telephone call.'

Grace was instantly alert. 'Who is it?' she asked.

It was rare for her to receive calls at the post house. Most people used her mobile number.

'Daniel. I did say I thought you were asleep but that I would check. I would have put him off only he said it was urgent.'

Grace dragged on her dressing gown. 'I'll be right down.'

'Use the extension in the kitchen, dear. Lovely night last night, wasn't it? Beattie and I haven't enjoyed ourselves so much for ages. We did enjoy your French song. I can't speak the language, but we both had a jolly good go at joining in.'

Amelia bustled away her face still wreathed in smiles while Grace tried to get her head together. What on earth could Daniel want at this time of a Sunday morning? He didn't need her to open up the surgery and it certainly wouldn't be a social call after last night's healthy exchange of views between them.

'Hello?' she asked still trying to clear her head. 'What's happened?'

'There you are.' Daniel's voice sounded perfectly ordinary. 'I need your help.'

'Is it the surgery? There hasn't been a break in has there?'

'No, nothing like that.' Daniel replied in an infuriatingly calm voice.

'Can't it wait until tomorrow?' Grace began to grow annoyed. It seemed Daniel had dragged her out of bed for no good reason.

'No, it has to be today. Can you be ready in about half-an-hour?'

'Where are we going?' Grace demanded.

'Wait and see.'

Grace was cut off before she could quiz Daniel further. Annoyed for not having been able to think up an excuse for turning down his invitation, Grace realised she had no option but to get dressed.

A pot of tea was still warm on the hob and she poured a cup and quickly made a round of toast. She was feeling hungry and last night's sumptuous dinner seemed a long time ago.

Fortified by the food and drink, Grace ran back upstairs. Hopefully there would be enough warm water left in the system for a quick bath. There were no shower facilities at the post house and the plumbing system was erratic, but Grace was pleased when a healthy trickle of water soon filled the bath.

There was no time to wash her hair, but the quick rinse left her feeling refreshed and more than ready to deal with Daniel. She wondered what his problem was and why it necessitated her presence so urgently.

A quick glance out of the window revealed that it was going to be a warm day. Grace chose to wear a short-sleeved blouse; a pair of lightweight trousers and a jumper, hoping her choice of clothes would fit the bill for whatever it was Daniel had in mind.

Before she had time to think further about where they were going, Amelia was calling up the stairs.

'Daniel's here. Are you ready?'

Grabbing up her handbag, Grace made her way downstairs. Like her Daniel had opted to dress casually. He was wearing jeans and an open necked check shirt.

He smiled. 'Sorry, to jump this on you at short notice,' he apologised, 'but we've only got until lunchtime.'

'What's this all about?' Grace demanded.

'Let's get in the car first, shall we?'

Soon they were driving out of the

village, through the rolling landscape that led deep into farmland. The road grew and meandered all over the place.

'Fun, isn't it?' Daniel grinned at her. 'Isn't there some sort of rhyme about the rolling Sussex rustic creating the rolling Sussex roads?'

'Possibly,' Grace murmured a reply.

'The first time I came out here I got hopelessly lost. It was dark and raining heavily. There was no-one I could ask for directions and I was lucky not to collide with a sheep that loomed up at me out of the mist. I drove around for hours. I tell you I was beginning to lose hope until I saw a light. I had visions of being lost forever. You know like in those horror films they show on late night television?'

'The dark does that to you,' Grace agreed before she remembered she really wasn't in the mood for making small talk with Daniel.

After Jason had brought her home she had tossed and turned in her bed until the small hours, then fallen into a deep sleep, only to be woken up by Amelia telling her about Daniel's telephone call.

'Where are we going?' Grace asked again.

'Ham Farm.'

'I've never heard of it.'

'Not many people have. A crusty old farmer used to live there. He made enemies of everyone so in the end he had no visitors and none of the tradesmen would call. After he died, his children sold the place and the new people who moved in renamed it. They had a lot of work on their hands, but they're winning.'

'Why are we going to visit them?'

'It was their dog I have been tending. You remember that emergency call out?'

'There have been several,' Grace replied.

'You're right. Anyway Bella is well on the way to recovery after giving birth to a litter of puppies.'

'Couldn't you have seen to her on

your own?' Grace was still puzzled. 'Sunday is my day off.'

'I thought you might like a trip out. Here we are.'

Daniel swung his car through a large five-barred gate and they drove down the tarmac drive.

'I must say, the surface is a whole lot better than the first time I came out here. I thought I'd done my suspension no good, I can tell you.'

The door to the farmhouse swung open and to Grace's surprise a man in a suit greeted them.

'Hello there.'

'Richard,' Daniel climbed out the car and greeted the man. 'This is Grace, my assistant.'

'Pleased to meet you. Sorry about the tight schedule, only I'm going back to London as soon as you're finished here. I've been called to a meeting, would you believe on a Sunday? City types are no respecters of weekends I am sorry to say. Come on in. It's only me here. Jenny went back to town last night with the children. Her mother is not well, so of course it's all happening at Ham's. Things will settle down I hope when we've properly moved in.'

'How's Bella?'

'Couldn't be better. I don't know what we would have done without your help. Bella decided to give birth the second night we arrived,' Richard informed Grace. 'It wasn't straightforward. Story of my life at the moment.' A cheerful smile crossed his face.

'Still I can't wait to get down here on a full time basis. With modern technology I don't need to be based in London. I can just as well run my consultancy from a barn as from a penthouse and prices down here are so much cheaper. It will be much healthier for the children too.

'Jenny's mother will be joining us as well, so that will be a relief. It'll mean Jenny won't have to keep abandoning ship here to drive up to see her at a moment's notice. Would you like some coffee?' Richard looked at his watch.

'Not if we're going to delay you,' Daniel replied.

'No trouble at all. I've got to make a couple of telephone calls. Go and see Bella while I get the percolator on. She's sunbathing outside with the last of her brood.'

There was an excited whining from a dog basket as Grace and Daniel approached. Bella wagged a lazy tail at them then went back to her snooze. A small bundle of golden fur lurched itself at Grace with all the ferocity of a guided missile.

'Whoa, steady on, old chap.' Daniel ducked as the soft body landed on Grace's feet and began to lick at her toes. 'You wouldn't believe he's the runt of the litter, would you?'

'Hello, you.'

Grace knelt down and tickled the soft fur at the back of the puppy's neck.

'Aren't you a beautiful boy?'

The recipient of her attention clearly agreed with her and set up an excited yapping before rolling over on his back.

'All that will have to stop,' Daniel said mock sternly, 'when we get you home.'

'Home?' Grace looked up from tickling the puppy's tummy.

'Yes.' There was a challenge in his hazel eyes.

'You mean as a replacement for Foxy?'

'Don't you like the idea?'

'I think it's a lovely one.'

'I've never been without a dog.' Daniel's voice was so soft Grace had to lean in to hear what he was saying. 'I had Foxy from a puppy and I thought we could train this little chap up as a sort of surgery pet. It would be good therapy and it might stop the visitors from eating too many biscuits,' he added with a smile.

'Like a pat a dog?' Grace asked, referring to the scheme that had been a great success in care and nursing homes.

'Exactly. Animals love all the extra attention and I thought it would make a sort of focal point and if I got delayed well, there might not be quite so many complaints if people were forced to wait. You see,' Daniel quirked an eyebrow.

'I believe,' Grace said slowly, 'that at last you're getting the hang of village life.'

'Is that a compliment?'

'Of a sort.'

'I need your approval first, of course. In the early days it might mean extra work for you. I'll help when I can and I'm sure the regulars will love him, as long as he follows house rules.'

A cold nose on her leg demanded Grace's attention.

'What do you think of the idea?' she asked the excited dog.

Her suggestion was met with much tail wagging.

'I think he likes it,' Grace said to Daniel.

It was warm on the patio and Grace shaded her eyes against the sun. She didn't feel tired any more and she was glad Daniel's call had got her out of bed. She hadn't been looking forward to a day of helping Andy out in the shop while Amelia and Beattie undoubt-edly would have talked about the best night they had had out in years.

'We have to take the puppy home today because as Richard told you, he's temporarily closing up the farm.'

'What's going to happen to Bella?' Grace asked looking at the puppy's mother.

'Richard is keeping her. She's incred-ibly gentle with the children and the new baby. It was actually the children's idea for us to have the last of the litter. All the others have gone to good homes so winners all round, wouldn't you say?'

'What shall we call him?' Grace asked.

Daniel picked up the puppy and he began to work his legs in a fervour of more excitement.

'How about Golden Boots?' he asked.

'Shortened to Goldie?' Grace sug-gested as the little face turned towards her.

'Goldie it is,' Daniel nodded.

'So, business done.' Grace looked round wondering where Richard was with the coffee.

'Not quite,' Daniel said.

'Did you bring me out here for another reason?' Grace joked. 'I hope you're not going to suggest we buy some sheep? I really don't think the surgery would be ready for a ram in reception.'

'My second reason to bringing you out her was to ask you to marry me,' Daniel said casually.

'What?' Grace choked down her surprise.

'Steady. Mind Goldie.'

Daniel dropped the dog back onto the ground. He immediately dashed back to the basket to where his mother was still sleeping.

'What did you say?'

'I think I just asked you to marry me, didn't I? That was my intention.'

'Why?'

'For the usual reason I suppose. Totally illogical I know, but I happen to have fallen in love with you.'

'You can't have done.'

'I think I know my own emotions,'

Daniel protested mildly. 'I admit it came as a bit of a surprise to me too, but there it is. I can't live without you. I can't live without a dog either come to that, but I'd give you top priority,' he added with a smile.

'You drove all the way out here to propose to me?'

'Yes, I did. It's a lovely setting, isn't it?'

'Lovely,' Grace echoed in a faint voice.

'You see, every time I try to get you on your own a constant stream of people decide to interrupt us. If it isn't Melissa, it's Jason or Charlie or even young Andy. It's been an absolute nightmare. I've wanted to tell you for ages that I think you're beautiful, kind hearted, just about the most wonderful girl I've ever met. You're a fighter too.

'Life dealt you a raw deal, but you didn't roll over and give in. You fought back. Everybody loves you. You can tell that by the way they've all been leaping to your defence. Some of the things I had said to me when you walked out of the surgery would have made your hair stand on end, but that's another story.'

Grace clutched some garden furniture and clung onto a wooden chair.

'You accused me of giving the surgery a bad name.'

'Charlie put me right on that one last night and I told you I only used it as an excuse to get you to leave for propriety's sake. Charlie accepted full responsibility for what happened and added a few other home truths about what he would do to me if I upset you ever again.

'I won't go into the details now, but it's really not the sort of respect I'd expect from a future brother-in-law.

'Still, given the circumstances I am prepared to make allowances. You know, this time I've great hopes for the deal he's doing with Jason. They've both grown up a lot recently. You'll never guess what,' Daniel went on with hardly a pause, 'Odile and Melissa are friends. I thought that would surprise you.'

'Daniel?' Grace held up a hand to stop him.

'Yes?'

'Can you please slow down?'

'Sorry. It's nerves. If I were a dog I'd probably be doing a Goldie on you. You know, running around. As it is, will you settle for a simple proposal? Er, I don't think you've said yes, have you?'

'There really is nothing between you and Melissa?'

'Scouts' honour. There never was, not even back in the mists of time when we were all young. She liked to pretend there was and I went along with her for a while for an easy life, but we've never been anything more than friends and we weren't engaged, not officially anyway. How about you and Jason?'

'He's a friend of my brother's, that's all.'

'I hate to rush you,' Daniel insisted, 'but Richard needs to go back to town and I suppose I should have a proper answer to my question. It's only polite, isn't it?'

'What question was that?' Grace pretended confusion. It was a lovely feeling seeing the uncertainty on Daniel's face and it would be fun to keep him on his toes for a few moments longer.

'Weren't you listening?' his voice rose in mild irritation. 'I asked you to marry me.'

'That question?' Grace teased.

'Yes, that question,' Daniel replied through gritted teeth.

'I can't answer for Goldie, of course,' Grace pretended to consider her answer, 'I mean we haven't asked him officially if he'd like to be the surgery dog, but my answer is in the affirmative.'

Hearing his new name, Goldie began to run round in circles again, barking ecstatically. Neither Daniel nor Grace took any notice of him as they looked into each other's eyes.

'I want to keep working even after we're married,' Grace insisted, 'I'm not about to turn into a subservient female.'

'I didn't for one moment imagine you would.'

'Coffee's ready,' Richard called through sticking his head out of the open kitchen window a few moments later. 'Oops, sorry,' he retreated back inside as he realised his two visitors were locked in an embrace on his patio and it looked as though the coffee might be cold by the time they were ready to drink it.

THE END